13

Also by Dan Elish:
The Attack of the Frozen Woodchucks

JASON
ROBERT
BROWN
&DAN
ELISH

LAURA GERINGER BOOKS
An Imprint of HarperCollins *Publishers*

Turn to page 202 for information on how to listen to an exclusive mp3
of Jason Robert Brown singing from the musical *13*.

13

www.harpercollinschildrens.com

Library of Congress Cataloging-in-Publication Data
Brown, Jason Robert.
13 / by Jason Robert Brown and Dan Elish.—1st ed.
p. cm.
Summary: Almost thirteen-year-old Evan Goldman learns what it
means to be a man when his parents separate and he and his mother move
from New York City to Appleton, Indiana, right before his bar mitzvah.
ISBN 978-0-06-078749-3 (trade bdg.)
ISBN 978-0-06-078750-9 (lib. bdg.)
[1. Interpersonal relations—Fiction. 2. Peer pressure—Fiction. 3. Bar
mitzvah—Fiction. 4. Divorce—Fiction. 5. Schools—Fiction. 6. Indiana—
Fiction.] I. Elish, Dan. II. Title. III. Title: Thirteen.
PZ7.B814193Th 2008   2008000777
[Fic]—dc22   CIP
                                                                         AC

Typography by Jennifer Rozbruch
1 2 3 4 5 6 7 8 9 10
❖
First Edition

Dedicated with love and gratitude to
Molly, Cassie, and John . . . and their mothers
—J.R.B. and D.E.

I GUESS it started with Angelina, the flight atten-
dant my father met on a flight from New York to L.A.
last year. I don't know the whole story. Maybe he
caught her eye while she was handing out pretzels?
Pretty much all I know is that on July 15 at 5:45 P.M.,
I left Central Park and came home to our apartment
to find Mom bawling on the sofa and Dad looking
sheepish by the terrace—sort of like he had just cut in
front of an old lady to snag a cab.

"Evan. Your father has some news."

Dad drew in a sharp breath. "It's really very sad."

I knew it: My grandmother had died. No, grand-
father. Wait, definitely my aunt, oh my god, my aunt

Elaine, it was going to be horrible.

"Your mother and I can't live together anymore."

I sat—more like collapsed—on our old blue easy chair, like I had taken a giant cannonball to my gut.

"What?" I said. It was all sort of hard to believe. My folks fought every once in a while, but it was a "Why can't *you* put dinner on the table for once?" kind of a thing, not "I hate you and don't want to be married to you anymore."

Anyway, the next thing I knew, we were all crying and hugging. Then, before I could catch my breath, my dad was heading to the door with his suitcase.

"I'll pick you up for dinner tomorrow at six," he said. "We'll talk, okay, buddy?"

And just like that I became one of those kids you see on those after-school specials: a guy who sees his dad once a week for dinner and every other weekend. Except I wasn't on TV. And by the time my dad had one foot in the hall, I was crying all over again.

And my mom? Well, she tried to be good, but it took only an hour before the bathroom door was closed, and I could hear her screaming from inside: "A STEWARDESS! IS HE KIDDING?"

My dad had made it sound mutual, like something they had agreed on together over their morning latte. But listening to my mom, I realized that it had been a one-sided decision—my dad had decided he couldn't live with my mom. And it began to sink in that, by extension, my father also wouldn't be living with me—not ever again. That night before bed, I punched out my pillow. Then I kicked in my closet door. You might say I was angry. You might say I was a lot of things—none of them good.

The next night at dinner, my dad said all the stuff you would expect. He never meant for it to happen. Life throws you strange curves. He loved me more than anything. I could see he was trying, but by the end of the meal I had tuned him out. Sure, each one of his so-called explanations sounded reasonable, but to my ears he was just spinning lines, desperate to get my forgiveness. Bottom line: My father was ditching me for some woman in polyester who dispensed peanuts across the friendly skies of America. It didn't matter that she turned out to be nice when I met her a few days later. By that point I had already made my decision. I hated her. And to tell the truth, I was starting to hate him.

"But you can't *really* hate him."

That's what Steve said. He was my best buddy. It was hard talking to him about the miseries of my home life, because he and my other best friend, Bill, were in a much more celebratory mood: Three days before all this happened, I had made contact with Nina Handelman's upper lip at Peter

Kramer's birthday party.

"How was her breath?" Bill said. "I bet her breath smells like candy."

"Whatever," I muttered.

"Evan, you can't *really* hate your own father," Steve repeated.

"Oh, yeah?" I said. "Sure I can."

"It's not biologically possible," Bill said. "He's your dad."

"I know he's my dad," I said. "But he took off. I mean, you should see my mom."

It was ugly. For the first few days after Dad left, she pretty much lived in her bathrobe, staring vacantly into space, wandering around the apartment, crying. On the fifth day, while she was halfheartedly attempting to make dinner, still in her bathrobe, I heard her mutter, "I've gotta get us out of here—we're not safe."

"Huh?" I said.

She forced a huge, fake smile.

"Never mind me, just talking to myself," she said. "More spaghetti?"

Later that night, I caught her crying again, this time on the phone to my aunt Pam. I didn't really listen much to what she was saying; I just heard the emotional roller coaster in the next room. Suddenly Mom's head popped into my doorway. "Hey, kiddo, guess what we're going to do?" It was the happiest she had sounded since Dad left. "We're moving to Indiana!"

She was grinning, ear to ear, like Dr. Teeth, even though her cheeks were still damp with tears.

"That's great, Mom," I said, and made a mental note to talk to Steve's mom about all of this. She was a shrink.

"Pam offered me a job!"

Aunt Pam had an antiques store. She sold about a chair a week. My mother had a doctoral degree in anthropology. Nothing was adding up.

"Mom, we can't go to Indiana. I've got school. And friends."

She looked at me, still cheerful, perky almost. "They've got schools in Indiana."

I went on, making my case. It was only five weeks before my first year in junior high. A few months before my thirteenth birthday.

But my mother would not be swayed; we were moving to Indiana! To be with Pam! Wasn't that great? I argued with her, but it was like talking to a boulder. An insane, grinning boulder. She wanted as far away from my dad as she could get. And I'm guessing she wanted to punish him a little bit, too. You know—if he didn't want her, he wasn't going to get me, either.

In the end, I had no choice. My dad tried to fight

it, even threatened with the lawyers, but he'd stacked the cards against himself: He had just left his wife for another woman, and he traveled almost every week for work. By the time he officially gave in, my mom had sold off half our stuff. Then one steamy, miserable day in early August, Steve and Bill and a few of Mom's friends came by to help load up the U-Haul and say good-bye.

"We'll keep in touch," Steve assured me.

"Tell you all about school," Bill said.

"Yeah, just stay away from Nina Handelman," I said halfheartedly. "Those lips are mine."

Bill shrugged awkwardly. "On a strictly literal basis, only the upper lip is yours."

Was he really going to move in on Nina Handelman the minute I left town? No way would he do that.

"Evan!"

My mom had just finished hugging Mrs. Lieber, our downstairs neighbor.

"Time to go, honey."

I looked at our apartment building—thirty stories, straight up. It had always seemed like nothing more than a tall mass of steel, brick, and glass. Suddenly it was home.

"In the car," Mom said.

It was hard to believe how fast my life had spun out of control. I thought of making one last-ditch attempt, throwing myself on the mercy of the court, begging to stay. I was beating all the other guys in Halo! Steve's dad got tickets to the Jets opener! Nina Handelman! But just like that, the feeling passed. I was old enough to know when a battle was lost. So I gave Steve a hug, slapped Bill's back, and walked to the car. All of a sudden I was blinking back tears. Not just because I was leaving, but because of who wasn't there to say good-bye. I knew Dad and Mom were at war, but I guess I still expected him to show up at the last minute, maybe even waving a court order that said I had to stay in New York. Instead I slouched into the passenger seat of Mom's old Volvo, depressed to the bone. I nodded out the window a final time—even Manuel, our doorman, had come out to wave good-bye. But still no Dad. And then Mom was in the seat next to me.

"Ready?" she said.

I just stared straight ahead and nodded. Forget my father. He and Angelina were probably in first class on some jet, bathing in a tub of champagne.

Or maybe not. As Mom inched the car down the street, I twisted around for one last look. And he was there! Getting out of a cab. Waving after the car. Running.

"Mom!" I said. "Stop!"

She sped up.

"Mom!"

She stopped.

But then I saw someone else get out of the cab, the early-morning sun catching her perfect younger-woman hair. Angelina.

"Forget it," I said.

Mom wrinkled her brow. "What?"

"Drive!"

Mom didn't have to be told twice. With a triumphant glance into the rearview mirror, she peeled down First Avenue like she was Jeff Gordon. I watched my dad run for a block, then stop, hands on his hips. He looked confused and sad.

That made two of us.

• • •

Our trip west wasn't any joyride. For starters, somewhere outside of Newark, the air conditioning broke down. It was ninety-five degrees. Then right as we entered Pennsylvania, the engine began making a horrible clanging noise, and continued doing it every five seconds for the rest of the trip. Then things got really bad. We were in Ohio when my mom brought it up, almost as an afterthought, half talking to herself.

"Once we're settled, we'll have to get to work finding you a rabbi for your bar mitzvah."

Clang, went the engine.

"My bar mitzvah?" I said. "Are you kidding? I'm

not having my bar mitzvah in Indiana."

It felt good to say it. I should have stopped there. But I kept going, not even sure where the words were coming from. "You want to drag me away from my *father*, fine, you do that, obviously it doesn't matter to you what I want. Well, I don't care what *you* want, and I'm not having a stupid bar mitzvah."

Clang.

Clang.

Clang.

My mother glowered at me, her face on fire with fury.

"You. Are. Having. Your. Bar mitzvah."

Clang.

Clang.

"Do you understand me?"

I gulped. We were going ninety miles an hour.

"You are having your bar mitzvah, Evan Goldman, and you are having it in Appleton, Indiana, with me and your aunt Pam, and that is the end of that discussion. Forever. Period. Are we very clear?"

Clang.

Clang.

"Yes, Mom."

We were silent for the rest of the trip.

Back in New York, I had taken two lessons with Rabbi Cohen and decided that Hebrew just wasn't my thing. I couldn't sing and I didn't know Exodus from Psalms. So I had begged my dad to skip the bar mitzvah and just throw me a big party. But now with Dad out of the picture, apparently the bar mitzvah was on again, and there was no one left to appeal to.

I looked out the window, exit after exit on the highway. Great. I could only imagine my first month at school. Everyone was already going to think I was some sort of weirdo fatherless New York Jewish freak.

What would they think when they heard me chant in Hebrew?

A HOUSE. We were going to live in a house. That, all by itself, was actually a pretty cool idea. Not worth moving to Indiana for, but since I had to go anyway, at least there would be a house. Big yards, grass, trees, quiet streets, and most important—space, lots and lots of space to stretch out, to leave my stuff everywhere, to have a bicycle AND a skateboard AND a scooter. I wasn't much excited about anything, but I was, I admit, a little excited about living in a house.

Apparently houses come in all sizes. Pam's, it turns out, is a Small House. A Small And Very Cluttered House. It wasn't an *actual* shack; she wasn't a tenant farmer or anything, but the life of a struggling antiques dealer, even in Appleton Indiana, does not provide for a large estate. There was a yard, a nice one with a big oak tree, and a cracked sidewalk that wound its way from a white picket fence to a yellow front door. But the house, even from my blurry viewpoint in the passenger seat of our clanging vehicle at eleven o'clock on the longest night of my life, was way tiny, and sort of run-down.

"Be nice," Mom whispered as she turned off the engine.

Before I could say anything, there was Pam, waving from the front porch, and a large dog running out to meet the car, barking and snarling.

Aunt Pam is not technically my aunt. She and my mom went to college together, and then Pam moved out here with her then-husband, Roy. That didn't last long, which you'd understand if you saw Pam now: short bowl-cut hair, corduroy shorts, flannel shirt, Birkenstocks. My dad always used to say that Pam looked like National Public Radio. After her marriage fell apart, she stayed in Indiana, got a big dog named Simon, bought a house, and opened her store. It had been twenty years since college, but she and Mom were still best friends.

"Ruth!" Pam called, and all but skipped into Mom's arms.

"Pam!"

I was still in the car, because Simon was pacing in front of the passenger-side door, drooling and growling.

"Don't be afraid, honey!" Pam yelled. "He only bites Republicans!"

I warily opened my door, and Simon jumped up and licked me, then immediately ran back to the front porch. I stretched my arms, unfastened my seat belt, and took the first step into my new life.

Even though the outside looked like something from the set of *Larry the Cable Guy*, the inside of the house was sort of wild. The foyer connected to a largish living room, small dining room, and kitchen. There were about twenty weird voodoo masks hanging on the walls, as well as these wood carvings of naked African women painted entirely in red. Near the dining room table was a rocking horse and a surprisingly realistic cactus made out of papier-mâché. Exotic mobiles and big plastic chickens hung from the kitchen ceiling. Side by side with the voodoo stuff, the living room was decorated with old road signs (one said "New York City, 695 mi"), a couple of wood stoves, and . . . no television. Anywhere.

"You're down here, Evan," Pam said.

I followed her into a small bedroom. It was pretty bare—just a dresser, a bed, and a little desk. I looked for an internet cable or even a phone jack. No luck. I didn't even bother wondering whether the house was wireless.

"This used to be my study," Pam said. She touched my shoulder. "You can decorate it however you like. Heavy metal posters. Pictures of girls. It's your space."

She was working very hard at being accommodating.

"Thanks," I said. "This'll be great."

Pam wiped a strand of hair out of her face, then gave me this super-concerned look. "This must be a very emotional time for you."

Well, yes, it was. And since I'd just been in the car with Psycho-Mom for the last fourteen hours, I wasn't in the best frame of mind to be discussing it.

"I'm fine," I said.

"Okay, then. But if you ever need someone to talk to . . . " For a moment I was scared Pam was about to ask if I wanted to join her art therapy class or something.

Mom called from across the hall. "Which bed should I take?"

"Take your pick," Pam called. "You're the guest."

We walked two steps and we were in the master bedroom. Pam's house was smaller than our New York apartment! Only two bedrooms, which meant that Mom and Pam would be sharing. And once again, the décor was, well, elaborate, with bright purple walls and four large paintings of some Chinese guy wearing a wig. There were two twin beds, one by a window, one by the far wall.

I have to imagine that Mom was having second thoughts, but she did her best to remain upbeat.

"This one by the window would be perfect," she said with a smile. "Evan. Help me unpack."

It was almost eleven thirty by then. I was completely overwhelmed and exhausted. I was hungry. Simon was following me around trying to get me to throw a disgusting old tennis ball covered with dog spit. As far as I was concerned, she could unpack her suitcase just fine by herself.

I helped her unpack.

• • •

The next day we went to a local department store to shop for what my mother thought were fun "boy" things for my room. I mostly stared straight ahead in a daze.

My cell phone buzzed. It was a text from Bill.

got both lips

My fingers were suddenly trembling so badly I typed back:

u kiss mgma?

Bill knew who I meant. He texted again:

made out at Jenny C's BM 8 mins!

I leaned back against a new washer-dryer set. At that point I wouldn't have minded throwing myself inside and setting the dial to "disappear."

Another text:

goin 2 the movies w her tonite!

"Say, Evan?" It was Mom, holding up two lampshades. "Which one do you like better?"

My second-best friend had horned in on my sort-of girl at Jenny Cohen's bat mitzvah, and my mother expected opinions on interior decoration?

"Evan?" she said.

I needed air.

"Okay," Mom called as I ran past household cleansers to the door. "I'm picking the green one!"

We got home at four, loaded down with lampshades, throw rugs, detergent, tube socks, trash bags, and a million other things I wished I could go through life never having to think about. Once I was done unloading the car, I went to my room, shut the door, and reached for *The Fellowship of the Ring*. I guess I was trying to block out the Midwest by losing myself in Middle Earth. Didn't work. Just before dinner, I heard the phone ring.

"Evan!" Pam called. "Your father!"

My dad! A voice from my real life! From the city of my birth! I was up from my bed like a shot. But as I opened the door, I stopped short. I looked around me. The weird African art. The papier-mâché cactus. The stupid plastic chickens! Why should I speak to the man whose raging libido had relegated me to a life in hell?

"Tell him I'm out," I said.

"But honey," Pam said, "I already told him you were here."

"Tell him he can talk to Mom!"

I slammed the door so hard, the New York highway sign in the living room crashed to the floor.

I'll spare you a detailed description of my next few days as a citizen of the Hoosier State. I guess it's important to say that Dad called every night before dinner and that each time I refused to talk, then gave my closet door a few swift kicks. I might've busted it off its hinges if I hadn't found a way to work off some of my rage. Pam had an old ten-speed that fit me perfectly. I spent a few days riding past homes and farms and more homes and more farms. As for stores? Well, for a guy who grew up in a city with all-night everything, there wasn't much. Pam lived a few blocks from Appleton's main street (actually called "Main Street") but the pickings were slim. There wasn't even a

Starbucks. Along with Pam's store, there was an ice cream parlor called Calvi's, a general store, an Italian restaurant, and an Army Navy. I guess if you wanted a chocolate sundae and a pair of fatigues, you were all set.

What the town lacked in shopping options it made up for in churches. Main Street was brimming with them. The First Presbyterians, the Methodists, the Unitarians, and the Lutherans—they had them all. There was only one house of worship that seemed to be missing.

When I realized there was no synagogue, I relaxed a little bit for the first time since I had arrived. After all, how was I going to have a bar mitzvah when there was no rabbi in town?

I think it was day seven post–New York when I came home from another long, boring bike ride to find Mom tooling around on the internet. (A dial-up connection, of course, but by that point I wasn't complaining. We were lucky Pam even had a phone.)

"Ev, come here, check this out!" my Mom said.

Out of the corner of my eye, I saw she was typing intently into a search box. The words I saw were:

`rabbi bar mitzvah western indiana`

I thought, Well, that's gonna come up empty.

"Oh, look!" she said. "This is perfect."

A web page was appearing: a picture of a building that looked more like a firehouse than a synagogue and a photo of an elderly guy with a long, gray beard. The caption said:

`Learn the Torah with Rabbi Weiner!`

Mom reached for the phone.

"What are you doing?" I said.

"Calling the rabbi."

"No, you aren't," I said.

"Evan," she said. "This is your religious education."

"I don't want a religious education! I want to go home!"

Mom ignored me completely.

"What do you even know about this guy?" I asked, looking over her shoulder at the screen.

"I don't know anything yet," Mom said. "That's why I'm calling him. Stop panicking. A rabbi's a rabbi."

"Some rabbis are child molesters."

"No, Evan, priests are child molesters." Mom nodded toward the screen. "Rabbis are nice."

I made a final stand. "I'm not going!"

"Oh, yes you are!"

"You can't make me!" I yelled.

Later that day, I found myself next to Mom in Aunt

Pam's old Subaru headed for my first haftorah lesson with Rabbi Herman Weiner. Forty-five minutes of silence later—hey, I was already freezing out my dad, so why not my mom too?—we drove around a corner and there was the building from the website. It turns out it really *was* a firehouse—an old one, now converted into the Cranston, Indiana, Community Center. Rabbi Weiner's office was on the second floor.

"Ah, you must be Evan!" he said when I walked in.

He was even older than his picture—I'm talking ancient, like he went to yeshiva with Moses. But with a single look my way, his face lit up like I was the first Jew he had seen in decades.

Mom pushed me forward. "Evan's so happy to meet you," she said.

I spent the next hour slogging through my haftorah, the ancient Hebrew text I was expected to chant at my bar mitzvah. It was excruciating. Rabbi Weiner leaned over me with his old-man breath, correcting my pronunciation. Then he told me I had to translate the entire thing into English and give a speech about what it all meant.

"A speech? Isn't the Hebrew enough?"

"You are becoming a man!" he croaked. "You must tell everyone about your journey!"

I didn't want to have a bar mitzvah. I didn't want to chant a haftorah. I didn't want to tell everyone about my journey. I wanted to throw myself under a truck.

"Evan's free every day until school starts," Mom said.

Rabbi Weiner smiled like he had just won the lottery. "Excellent! We'll meet again tomorrow!"

3

Ruth Goldman cordially invites you
To share in the blessings of the children of Abraham.
Saturday, September 23rd
When her son,

Evan David Goldman,

Embraces the Torah as a Bar Mitzvah

There was day at some point in the next week when I
came out of my lesson with Rabbi Weiner and Mom
was sitting in the car looking completely burned out.

So I spoke to her for the first time in days.

"What's wrong?"

"I don't know, kiddo," she said. "This is hard, doing a bar mitzvah out here. Maybe your dad's right and you should do it back in New York."

Joy! Justice! I suddenly couldn't wait to call Steve and Bill to break the good news.

But then disaster. Mom found out that Angelina had moved into our old apartment with Dad. All of Appleton heard the screaming that night. And that was the end of my New York bar mitzvah. Even worse, I suddenly wasn't allowed to invite a single member of Dad's family! Furthermore, she would not accept one penny ("NOT ONE PENNY!") from my father for the party. He could keep his tainted money. She would do the whole thing herself!

The situation sucked. And I had no one to talk to. Bill was too busy sucking face with Nina to talk about anything else, and Steve seemed distant the couple of times we spoke, like I was already some landmark on the road fading from sight in the rearview mirror.

"By the way," he told me the last time we talked. "Aaron Siegel's bar mitzvah's a week before yours."

"Yeah," I said. "So?"

Aaron Siegel was the richest kid in our class. He was having his bar mitzvah at the Pierre Hotel, and his father had hired Beyoncé to sing the Hatikvah.

"Well, the week after, his dad is flying some of the guys down to their condo in Florida. Isn't that cool?"

You know in books where they say a person's skin goes cold? Well, that's what happened to me. Like ice. Nobody was going to miss out on a free trip to Florida—especially not if the option was to take a plane and a bus to attend my bar mitzvah in nowheresville Appleton.

"Yeah," I choked. "Cool."

"It's just that I'm really torn about what to do," Steve began.

I cut him off. "Don't worry about it, dude," I said. "Have fun."

"For sure?"

I don't think I had ever heard anyone sound so relieved.

"Yeah," I said. "For sure."

"Thanks, dude," he said. "We'll talk later, okay?"

I sort of knew that we wouldn't—not soon anyway. He had New York things to do. And me? I had this:

Please join us for a reception afterward:

The Methodist Church
Main Street, Appleton
Basement Community Room

So for a quick recap, here's how things stood:

I wasn't talking to my dad.
I was grunting monosyllabically at my mom.
I was drifting apart from my New York
*   buddies.*
I was being bar mitzvahed by a rabbi we
*   found online.*
I was celebrating in the basement of a church.

Could anything possibly go right?

• • •

Thank god for Simon, that lovable, slobbering monster of a dog. It was because of him that I finally made a friend in Appleton. It was week two of my sentence in Hoosier jail. Simon and I were outside one morning playing fetch with one of Pam's naked figurines. After a few throws, Simon jumped the picket fence and dropped the statue in front of this skinnyish girl with her face buried in a book.

"Hey there, doggie!" she said.

Simon started licking her hands and barking. She scratched under his chin, then looked my way.

"You must be Evan," she said.

"I must?"

"Pam told me you were here."

She wrestled the figurine from Simon's mouth,

cocked her arm, and hurled it into the woods. Then I noticed the book she was reading—most girls are reading books about horses or guys named Chad; this girl was reading *The Corrections*. I was impressed— not only was this girl well-read, but she had a major league throwing arm.

"Did I just throw a naked lady?" she asked me.

We both started laughing.

As Simon tore after the figurine, I took a closer look. I had expected every girl in the Midwest to be some blond, blue-eyed, corn-fed beauty, but this girl wasn't that at all. She had long brown hair that fell straight into her face. Her eyes were small and kind of close together, like she was scrutinizing you. Her knees pointed in toward each other. On the plus side, she had a very nice, welcoming smile. Not to mention the beginnings of a real figure. My hormones gave her a tentative thumbs-up.

"What did Pam tell you about me?"

She smiled. "She said your parents just split up, you're too smart for your own good, angry at the world, and you could use a friend."

Before I even had a second to respond, the girl said, "Want to come to the library with me? It's not much, but they have a new room of DVDs."

"I will," I said, "on one condition."

"What?"

"You have to tell me your name."

Her name was Patrice.

It turned out that Patrice's parents had split too, except that she lived with her dad. Over the next few days, she showed me around town (what little of it there was) and introduced me to some classic movies. Patrice seemed to like movies better if they were in black and white.

She came with me the day I checked out the Methodist church. When we walked in, the basement was filled with a bunch of folding tables, like it was set up for bingo. In the corner was an upright piano that they probably used for square dances. The whole place smelled like old cottage cheese. I was miserable—this was the worst place you could possibly pick to have a party.

"Look at the bright side," Patrice said. "It won't look so bad with these tables folded up and some decorations. It's actually a pretty big space."

Which is when it hit me. How would I fill that space? If I was going to have this bar mitzvah in the middle of nowhere, who in the world would come? At that point I had a list of four: my mom, Pam, Patrice, and the rabbi.

I needed more friends.

But how? The only other neighbor my age I knew about was this curly-headed kid named Archie who lived across the street. Pam said he had some sort of really bad muscle disease and needed crutches to get around. Every once in a while I'd catch him staring at me through the window. Apparently he and Patrice were friends, but when I asked her about him, she just said he was complicated. I didn't know what that meant, but I thought he was pretty spooky, so I didn't push it.

Aside from Archie, Patrice's main buddies were her old movies and long novels. Clearly she wasn't going to be any help getting people to my bar mitzvah. If I wanted any kind of party at all, I had to find a way to get in with the Appleton in crowd. And the more I mulled it over, the more I knew what that meant: I had to meet Brett.

Practically every adult I met at first in town had mentioned Brett. "You're going into seventh grade," they'd say. "You must know Brett Connelly." Or "If you like football, you're gonna like Brett! He's going to play in States one year." Or "You know who you should meet? That Connelly boy!" The more I heard about him, the more he began to seem like a Mafia don—if you got in good with him, you were set. If you were in his crowd, you were cool.

I was hoping I could just bump into him one day, but our paths never seemed to cross. Finally, about a week before the start of school, Patrice and I were at

Calvi's sharing a sundae when she started quizzing me on my haftorah.

"Okay," she said. "Let's hear it. Whip off a few lines."

Just as I opened my mouth and began clumsily declaiming, "Koh-amar . . . ," the door swung open. And in he walked.

Brett. All blond, all muscle, a smile with more teeth than I had ever seen in one mouth in my life. Beside him were two goony-looking guys, one tall and pimply, the other short with a pushed-in face. Two girls brought up the rear: the first blond and blue-eyed and perky and giggly; the second dark-haired, a little taller, a little heavier.

"Chocolate sundae, my man!" Brett called.

Mr. Hanrady lit up like a ten-year-old with a new Game Boy when Brett walked into the store.

"You got it, QB!"

To be honest, I could see why Mr. Hanrady was so stoked. There was something about Brett—a swagger that made you want to be near him. He was actually magnetic, like they say about movie stars.

"What jerks," Patrice whispered.

This was a running theme with Patrice—anyone who was cool was a jerk. Everything could be going great and suddenly she'd get quiet, just giving some random kid the evil eye. That's what she was doing now, staring down the dark-haired girl with a really uncomfortable intensity. I didn't get it. Sure, Brett seemed cocky—with no prompting, he was telling Mr. Hanrady how he was going to lead the Quails to victory over the Thunderhawks in the first game of the season—but he didn't seem like a bad guy.

"What's wrong with him?" I asked Patrice. "He seems okay to me."

Before she could answer, something went *thwap* against my back—a rolled-up napkin. Across the room, the two goons were giving Brett high fives.

"Nice throw, Brettmeister!" the tall, pimply goon called.

"Bull's-eye!" said the short goon.

"Hey, Brain!" Brett called.

I blinked. "What?"

"That would mean you," the short goon said.

I glanced at Patrice. She rolled her eyes.

"Brain?" I said. "I'm the Brain?"

Brett nodded. "You're from New York City, right? You must be the Brain."

Somehow Brett seemed to know who I was. It was kind of exciting, the idea that people had been talking about me before they had even met me.

The dark-haired girl looked unhappy. She screwed up her brow.

"Why is he the Brain? Is he supposed to be smart?"

The blond girl giggled and squeezed Brett's arm.

Brett walked closer to me. I closed my bar mitzvah practice book and covered it with a napkin. Sure, my goal was eventually to invite Brett and all his friends to the party. But for all I knew, I was the first Jew any of them had seen outside of a *Seinfeld* rerun. Friends first, yarmulkes later.

"You play football, Brain?"

I was shocked. Was this some sort of a test? If so, I didn't want to fail it. The fact of the matter was that Rabbi Weiner was probably a better football player than I was.

"A little. More basketball."

"I got it!" the tall goon said. "Maybe the Brain can join the cheerleaders."

The short goon found this hilarious, to the point that he began to do a little fake cheer, pretending to be me, I guess. The blond girl giggled. The dark-haired girl smirked. When the tall goon started chanting along, Brett decided he had heard enough.

"Shut up, barf bags! You know, Fudge, we do need a new wide receiver."

Apparently the short goon's name was Fudge. "Hey, *I'm* the go-to guy! What are you talking about?"

Brett winked at me. "Love to make my boy nervous."

Suddenly the blond girl jumped up, as if from out of a trance.

"Oh, oh, oh!"

"What?" said the dark-haired girl.

"I love this song!"

Some perky pop thing sung by a girl from the Disney Channel was blaring out of Mr. Hanrady's radio. Suddenly the blonde was jumping and singing along, then writhing on the floor, kicking over Patrice's head and spinning around. I mean, I guess she was a good dancer—it was hard to judge: I had never seen anything like it. When she finished, she lay on the floor, spread out like Jesus on the cross, utterly spent. Brett cheered, then picked her up and carried her over his head.

"Ladies and gentlemen! I give you Kendra Peterson! Look out, *American Idol*!" He turned to me. "Isn't she the greatest, Brain?"

I wouldn't have said she was "the greatest." But she was certainly something. And I needed friends.

"She rocks!" I said.

"Oh, Jesus," Patrice whispered.

Brett tossed another napkin my way, then laughed sort of affectionately.

"Good taste, Brain," he said, and turned back to his table.

After that, he and his gang left us pretty much

alone. They ate their ice cream, we ate ours. But even while I was keeping up my end of the conversation with Patrice, I couldn't help noticing some of the dynamics at their table. From the way the dark-haired girl (whose name, it turned out, was Lucy) was hanging on Brett's every word, it was pretty clear she liked him as much as Kendra did. And Fudge made no secret of the fact that he had a major thing for Lucy. He even jumped up on the table and did this wild dance in her face, all arms and legs, until she shouted, "Get away from me, Fudge!"

It wasn't long before Patrice and I finished our sundaes. Since we had a date back at her place to watch another old movie, we decided to get going. But on the way out the door, something surprising happened.

"Hey, Brain." Brett swiveled around in his chair. "Want to hang at the quarry tomorrow? A couple of us are going swimming."

I looked at Patrice. "That sounds cool, right?"

Lucy turned quickly. "Not *her*, Brett. She can't come." She smirked at Patrice. "Nothing personal, of course."

I could tell that Patrice was trying as hard as she could to pretend she didn't care. But I could also see the hurt in her eyes. Clearly she and Lucy had some major history.

"I wouldn't go with you anyway," she said, then

pushed through the door to the street. As for Brett, he ignored the entire exchange.

"We'll meet here after lunch?" he went on. "Sound like a plan?"

I thought of Patrice stewing outside. I thought of the large empty basement of the Methodist church. I turned to Brett.

"Count me in!"

MY MOM and the rabbi had been on my case about writing my big bar mitzvah speech, but I kept putting it off. Finally even Patrice asked when I was going to start working on it, since the whole thing was only a month away. So I sat down and tried to get something on paper.

Being a Man, by Evan David Goldman

Thank you, rabbi. Thank you, mom. Thank you, Pam. Thank you, good people of Appleton.
I am now going to talk about my journey to manhood. That journey began when I was

*but a small fetus, growing in my mother's
womb. Nine long months I gestated, and
finally out I came. But was I a man yet? No, I
was not. First I had to be a baby. In my first
year, I threw up a lot and cried. Next I became
two. And so went my journey to manhood.*

It took me forty-five painstaking minutes to write
and five glorious seconds to rip to shreds. I'd have to
try again later. Besides, I had more important things
than manhood on my mind. After lunch I pulled on a
T-shirt and bathing suit and headed for the door.

"Have fun with that Connelly boy," Pam called. "I
hear he's quite a young man."

Incredible. Brett was such a big deal in town that
even Pam was impressed.

"I will," I said.

"Call if you're going to be late for dinner," Mom
reminded me.

I grunted.

"And careful at the quarry," Pam said. "Some
parts of it are shallow."

I dashed out before they could say anything else.
But when my foot hit the front porch, I stopped cold,
heart pounding. I looked in every direction, trying to
make sure Patrice wasn't anywhere in the area. I knew
if she saw me heading out to meet Brett and the gang,

she'd feel terrible. So I cut across the front yard of the house across the street and made for the shortcut to town that Patrice had showed me. I was so busy thinking ahead to the coming afternoon that I didn't see him until I was about five feet from his living room window. But suddenly there he was—Archie, wearing old Spiderman pajamas, staring out the window looking at me. He raised his hand in a Vulcan salute and waved for me to come inside. I didn't know what to do: Should I change my plans and spend the afternoon watching *Star Trek* episodes or something? Wouldn't that be the right thing to do? Who cares about the cool kids coming to your bar mitzvah when there's a lonely sick kid across the street who wants to be your friend?

I kept running and didn't even wave back.

By the time I got to Calvi's, Brett and the gang were already waiting. For a second I worried that they'd be pissed. Instead, Brett flashed this giant smile.

"Yo, everyone!" he said. "It's the Brain! Let the festivities commence!"

Just like that, all bad thoughts about Patrice and my sick neighbor catapulted straight out of my head. I mean, could it be any clearer? Somehow Brett Connelly had decided I was cool! And as Brett went, so went his girls and goons.

We started walking. I had come in on the middle of

a conversation about a movie that was coming to the mall in a couple of weeks.

"*The Bloodmaster*!" Fudge said. "It's supposed to be awesome!"

"I saw the preview last night!" said the tall goon, whose name was Eddie. "Showed this big, ugly freak with teeth like lawn-mower blades munching off a lady's leg!"

"Awesome!" Brett said, and pumped a fist.

Pretty soon we reached a narrow path that angled up into thick woods.

I looked around but didn't see any water.

"Are we close?" I asked.

Eddie gave my shoulder a shove. "Come on, Brain. We gotta hike!"

Brett and his goons pushed ahead. I tried to keep up, but before I knew it, I was back with Kendra and Lucy, panting and sweating, while the boys were racing up the long hill.

"Hey, Brett!" Eddie called. "Check out the Brain—sucking wind like my grandma's grandma!"

I saw Brett in the distance, glancing back with a grin. "Too hard for you, Brain?"

"No," I called up. "I'm cool!"

Kendra laughed.

"It's worth it once we get there," she said. "And the path levels out over that ridge."

Lucy was last, moving without any real ambition at all, just sort of dragging herself up the path.

"Ken?" she said. "If Brett goes out with me, maybe you can go out with Fudge."

Kendra laughed. "Why is Brett gonna go out with you?"

"I don't know, I'm just saying. I mean you were gone all summer."

"I was at camp for three weeks," Kendra said.

Lucy frowned. "But while you were away, we spent a lot of time together."

Kendra didn't seem concerned. "So what? Since I've been back, he's been calling me and texting me and all into me."

"Fine," Lucy said. "But it's weird that you guys have been spending all this time together and he hasn't asked you out yet. Not officially, anyway."

"Shut up! He will!"

Lucy smiled. "Okay. But just so you know, Fudge will be waiting."

Kendra started walking faster. She turned to me and said, "Don't listen to her. She's a cow."

We caught up to the boys at a clearing. Suddenly we were all standing on the edge of a cliff. About twenty feet below was the quarry itself, two hundred feet across, one hundred feet wide, and surrounded by towering pine trees that reflected off the dark blue water.

"Whoo-hoo!" Brett shouted. "They don't have water like this in New York, do they, Brain?"

I was floored—I admit it. "They sure don't."

"Let's do it!" yelled Eddie.

Before I knew it, everyone was taking running leaps into the quarry. First Eddie, then Brett, then Fudge, breaking the peaceful stillness of the afternoon with loud splashes and epic yells. Kendra and Lucy held hands and jumped together, screaming and laughing at the same time.

Boom! Splash!

Just like that, I was the only one left on the cliff.

"Come on, Brain!" Brett called.

I glanced over the edge. The water was about twenty feet down. Brett, Eddie, Fudge, Kendra, and Lucy looked like a gang of otters, treading water below me. Suddenly my heart was pounding pretty hard.

"He's scared!" Lucy called.

Fudge found that hilarious. Then again, I was beginning to discover he found everything hilarious as long as someone else was the butt of the joke.

"What's the matter, Brain?" he called. "Used to jumping into those New York City sewers?"

I could not move. Every second I stood there just made it worse. Where was the lifeguard? And where were those shallow parts Pam warned me about? And who was gonna call the ambulance?

"Brain, you're not gonna die!" Eddie called.

"Scared!" Fudge and Lucy chanted. "Scared! Scared!"

It was too bad Lucy hated him, because they seemed like the perfect couple, uniquely matched to raise a family of jerks.

"Leave him alone, guys!" Kendra said.

"Come on, Brain," Brett called. His good cheer was quickly turning to impatience. "Jump already!"

What could I do? I was terrified. But I was stuck. I pulled off my T-shirt, took a few small steps toward the edge of the cliff, and peeked over.

"My god!" Lucy called. "You're such a fraidycat!"

Next thing I knew, that became the chant: "Fraidycat! Fraidycat!"

I hadn't been called that since I was four, but the words were effective. All right, I thought, if nothing else, my parents will have to get back together for my funeral. I took a few steps away from the edge. "Come on, you coward," I told myself. "Just do it! Do it for . . . do it for Nina Handelman!" No, that didn't work—I just pictured her making out with Bill.

"Jump, Brain!" Brett called.

Now he was angry. And I really didn't want Brett to be angry. Next thing I knew, I was running full out for the water. Yes, I wanted to pull up short with every pore of my being. But I knew that if I stopped, I'd never find the guts to try again. And boom! I sprang off the edge, and suddenly there I was, grabbing serious air.

"Ahhhhh!" I cried.

The water rushed up to meet me. I went under hard, then kicked like a wild man for the top. But as soon as I snagged a lungful of air, my perspective flipped. There were my new friends, smiling, framed by this gorgeous scenery. With a couple more deep breaths, it dawned on me: I hadn't drowned! The water was great!

"Yee ha!" I shouted.

"Hey, Brain!"

It was Eddie, sending a wave of water right into my face. I jumped on top of him and dunked him. That started an enormous splash fight. Then Brett yelled, "Come on!" and we all swam to the other side of the quarry. Then we swam back, lay on some rocks, and got dried by the sun. To tell the truth, I couldn't remember the last time I had felt so good.

It would have been the perfect afternoon, if only it had stopped right there. But then we all started talking, or I guess I should say *they* all started talking, since I didn't really know any of the people they were talking about. I tried to pay attention, but I couldn't keep track of who was on what team or who was making out with whom. At some point, I realized everyone was cracking up about something, and Fudge jumped up and yelled, "Who am I?" He got on all fours and began to snort. Everyone was suddenly hysterical laughing and Lucy waved an arm and shouted, "Peter Primoff! Peter Primoff!" and Brett winked at me and said, "Fatter than a Macy's Parade float, Brain. You'll see." Then Lucy did her impression of her neighbor who had a lisp, Eddie imitated the sixth-grade French teacher, who apparently barked like a dog in the middle of her sentences, and Brett took a shot at a kid on the football team whose voice cracked a lot. Since I didn't know any of these people, it was easy to laugh along without really knowing who I was laughing at. But when Fudge began to clump along the rocks like he was walking with crutches? It got a little bit uncomfortable. And when he raised his hand in a Vulcan salute? Well, everything was happening so quickly. I could have defended Archie, I guess, but I didn't really know him. Anyway, it was just harmless goofing off, right?

Before I could get my bearings, Eddie was on his feet. First he knitted his brow so his face looked deadly serious. Then he walked knock-kneed across the rocks, pretending to read a book. Then he looked up as if out from under a pair of granny glasses, and he spoke in this pinched sort of voice: "No, no, no!

The United States Constitution was signed in 1787!"
Then he pretended to trip. I wish I could tell you I
didn't laugh, but it was in fact a surprisingly good
impression of Patrice.

"Stop! I'm laughing too hard!" Lucy said. "She's
such a loser!"

"What a nerd," Eddie said.

Fudge wagged his head. I laughed. I kept laughing.
I figured if I just kept laughing, the whole thing might
blow over.

"Say, Brain?" Brett was talking to me. I stopped
laughing. "What's up with you and Patrice anyway?"

Just like that, everything got super quiet. And not
quiet like in New York, where there's the reliable
background hum of traffic and construction. No, this
was deadly still like the world had stopped and was
waiting for my answer. A lone bird chirped in the
woods across the quarry.

"Patrice?" I said finally. My voice nearly broke.

"Yeah," Eddie said.

"Are you two friends?" Brett asked.

I swallowed hard and waved a hand.

"Patrice? Nah, she just lives next door."

Brett smiled. "I told you, Fudge."

Eddie laughed and jumped back in the water.
"Fudge thought you two were, like, going out."

Brett leaned back on the rocks. "The Brain knows

better than to hang out with a geek girl."

I felt my face flush. Lucy looked at me. "Yeah, sure he does."

Fudge pushed Lucy into the water, and within seconds Patrice had disappeared, completely forgotten.

"EVAN?"

Some people are cool and some people aren't. That's just the way life plays out.

"It's Patrice. Where are you?"

And I think, really, that being cool is just a matter of wanting to be cool.

"I can't believe you're not answering your phone."

Not just wanting it, but wanting it *enough*.

"I thought you were coming over tonight to watch Singin' in the Rain.*"*

Enough to say that maybe this thing I thought I liked isn't as good as I thought it was, because the cool people don't like it.

"*I know you're all busy with Brett, but you could call.*"

Like, okay, say I love chocolate, and I bring chocolate to lunch every day. And all the cool kids hate chocolate.

"*I made popcorn and everything.*"

But now I find out that they all love celery, and I don't like celery at all.

"*Anyway, we've got to get busy on your bar mitzvah speech, so just tell me when you want to do that.*"

Now I'm not gonna be cool just because I stop eating chocolate. That's wanting something a *little*, not wanting it *enough*.

"*I'm around all day tomorrow.*"

If I want to be cool, then I have to step it up: I have to love celery. Not just eat it, but love it.

Throw away the chocolate, love the celery.

"*Anyway, call me, you dork. I won't start the movie until I hear from you.*"

And if I can't do that, maybe I don't want it *enough*.

• • •

The next day was cloudy and cold. I was sitting on an old couch in Patrice's basement rec room, staring at an empty screen on her laptop.

"I don't know what to write," I said. And it was true. Every time I thought about this speech, I just went blank. I had no idea what becoming a man meant. I just wanted to be a kid.

"Just write anything."

I typed:

anything

Patrice sighed. "Fine, let's do something else."

"We can watch that movie if you want." I wasn't really in the mood to see *Singin' in the Rain* right then, but I was feeling bad about blowing her off the night before.

Patrice brightened. "Oh, yay! Okay, wait, let's go make more popcorn."

She jumped off the couch and ran up the stairs. I closed the laptop and followed her into her kitchen.

"So what happened last night anyway?" she asked, taking the cellophane off a package of microwave popcorn.

"I'm sorry about that—I just couldn't call." Lie. "I mean, first we got completely stranded at the quarry," lie, "and then my cell phone died," lie, "and by the time I got home, it was too late to call you." Lie.

"Oh."

Patrice got that hurt look again. She pushed the buttons on the microwave. "So what did you guys do anyway?"

"Well, after the quarry we went over to Eddie's house and his mom got pizzas for all of us. Then Fudge got this idea."

The kitchen was beginning to smell like butter.

"Oh, yeah?" I could tell Patrice was trying like mad not to be judgmental about my hanging out with Brett. "What was it?"

I told the next part of the story really fast. "It was just getting dark. So he said that we should stand on the side of the road, and when a car came around the corner and caught us in its headlights, we should pretend to be beating Eddie up. Then we should scatter and Eddie should fall to the grass like he was really hurt."

Patrice shot me a funny look. "What was the point of that?"

"I don't know," I said defensively. "You know, to scare the guy in the car."

"So you did it?"

"Well, I told them it sounded like a dumb idea." Lie. "I just wanted to go home." Lie. I shrugged. "Brett's a pretty hard guy to refuse."

Patrice's funny look took on a harder edge. "You know, he's not God, Evan."

For some reason I laughed. I mean, I knew she was right. But on the other hand, she was also wrong. Around Appleton, Brett was as close to a human deity as there was. Anyway, by that point I was really sorry I had started the story, but with Patrice leaning back on the kitchen counter, waiting, I had to finish.

"So a minute later, we saw headlights coming and all of us pretended to beat the crap out of Eddie. Then we ran for the hedges—the girls, too."

Patrice's eyes went wide. "Did the car stop?"

I nodded and just blurted out the rest of it. "Eddie really played his part, too. He held his stomach, moaned and said, 'My stomach. My face,' and stumbled off to his house. Then the guy in the car followed Eddie up the path asking if he could help. By that point, Eddie couldn't take it anymore. He started laughing and ran like a maniac toward the woods. Next thing I knew, we were all hysterical."

The microwave went *ding*. Patrice ignored it.

"What did the guy in the car do?"

I pulled out the bag of popcorn. "I don't know, he was all 'You rotten kids!' or something. We were too busy cracking up."

Patrice wrinkled her brow in this way that made her look a little bit like Mrs. Eckfeldt, my second-grade teacher at PS 194. "Why were you cracking up?"

Even though I had told Patrice everything, I had left out something crucial: how it all *felt*. The truth was that once we started to pretend to beat up Eddie, it was exciting. And when the car actually stopped and the guy got out to help? It was a rush. Just because it's a stupid prank doesn't mean it's not fun. It felt good to be one of the gang, feeling like we had pulled something off.

"I guess it was pretty stupid," I said.

"You think?" Patrice asked. Before I could respond, she took the popcorn from me and poured it into a bowl. "Oh, this is all burned! It's ruined."

I was starting to get really annoyed at her—I mean, who needed a schoolmarm for a friend? On the other hand, part of me knew she was right. The prank *had* been stupid. And as much fun as it turned out to be, I had really gone along only because I felt I had to. In any case, I didn't want the whole afternoon to be ruined. What I needed right then was to smooth things over. So I took two brownish pieces of popcorn, stuck them under my nose, and curved up my lip to make a popcorn mustache. Pretty dumb, but it broke the tension. Patrice giggled. Then she took a piece and threw it at me. Hit me right on the forehead.

"You're an idiot," she said.

I didn't know if she was kidding or talking about the prank. But I laughed.

"You too!"

Then I threw my mustache right back at her, and next thing I knew, we were having a giant burned-popcorn fight, laughing our heads off. Cleaning up a few minutes later, we were both careful not to mention Brett or the prank. But later on, we sprawled out on the ratty couch in her rec room to watch the movie with a fresh batch of unburned popcorn. I felt like I had to get something out of the way.

"You know, I think I can get them all to come to my bar mitzvah. That's cool, right?"

I brought up the subject right when Gene Kelly was doing this fantastic dance number around a bunch of lampposts, hoping I could slip in the news without Patrice noticing.

"Huh?" she said.

"Brett and the gang," I said. "I think I'm going to invite them."

Patrice paused the film. Suddenly Gene Kelly was frozen in space, an umbrella upside down in his hand.

"If that's what you want," Patrice said. "But they're just gonna act stupid and ruin the whole party."

I sighed. When I was with Brett and his gang, I had fun. When I was with Patrice? I got lectures.

"What is it with you and them anyway?"

Patrice leaned back on the couch. "Ask Lucy and Kendra. It might surprise you to know that we were friends when we were younger."

I couldn't quite picture that. "What happened?"

Patrice shrugged. "The minute we hit middle school, I suddenly didn't wear the right jeans. Or say the right things. I didn't smoke. It was mostly Lucy. She shut me out first, and Kendra and the others followed right along."

"Wow," I said. "That's crazy."

And yet it wasn't crazy. Spending a day with Kendra and Lucy made it all too obvious that Patrice didn't fit in with them. But looking at Patrice, still filled with hurt and anger, I wished that I could do something to fix it.

"So?" Patrice said. "Wanna finish the movie?"

I pressed the remote, and Gene Kelly swung around the lamppost and splashed in a puddle. He made it all look so easy.

● ● ●

The week before the start of school went by in a blur. What started as a day at the quarry with Brett and his gang turned into a whole string of plans that took up a lot of my time. Eddie, Fudge, Kendra, and Lucy were his main gang, but there were five other kids—Ryan, Nicole, Bridget, J.D., and Seth—who came along sometimes. Mostly we hung around Calvi's, playing video games and eating ice cream, but there was also a night at the movies, a state fair, and a minor league ballgame. All this in addition to my daily trips to Cranston to suffer with Rabbi Weiner. So I guess I just didn't have a whole lot of time to see Patrice, and the couple of times we did get together, it was awkward. I mean, we tried to pretend that everything was the same as it was before I had started to hang with Brett: We went to the library, we sat in her basement and watched movies. We had some laughs, but every time I had to leave, she could tell I was going to hang with the kids she hated, and as hard as she tried, she couldn't stop the hurt from showing. She also couldn't stop the rants about how stupid or how mean they were, or how they were going to ruin my bar mitzvah. So I guess I took the easy way out. I'm not exactly proud of it, but after a few days, when I saw Patrice's number on my caller ID I stopped picking up. At first she just called more. Then it tapered off. She got the point eventually. After a couple of days, she stopped calling entirely.

A few days before school began, I found myself sitting in Pam's living room addressing bar mitzvah invitations. To my amazement, I had a group of kids to invite. Here was my list:

Brett Connelly
Eddie Jones
Malcolm "Fudge" Venter
Lucy Abendroth
Kendra Peterson

J. D. Canaday
Nicole Willis
Seth Ashley
Bridget Keller
Ryan Ritchie
Patrice DeCrette

I got out Pam's old white pages, looked up their names, and copied each name and address as neatly as I could onto the fancy envelopes my mom had bought for the occasion. After that, Simon and I walked down the block to the mailbox. But this strange thing happened when I opened the slot to drop in the invites. The first ten envelopes slid right on down the chute, but I just couldn't mail Patrice's. It was like it was glued to my hand. Not literally, of course, but suddenly my heart was pounding and I was frozen. I mean, how awkward would it be if she came? She hated them. They hated her. Why put myself through that on the most important day of my life?

And then I had this really terrible thought. What if Brett and his gang found out Patrice was coming and then refused to come themselves? I remembered Lucy and Patrice's exchange at Calvi's the first time I had seen them together. Then I remembered how Eddie had made fun of Patrice at the quarry. And then I had the final thought—the biggie. I mean, I was still way too pissed to talk to him, but what if Dad came to my bar mitzvah anyway? What if he walked into the basement of the Methodist church and no one was there except for my mom, Pam, Patrice, and the rabbi we found online?

I closed the mailbox, slipped Patrice's invite back into my pocket, then called for Simon and ran home.

And then, before I knew it was happening, it was Labor Day, and summer vacation was over.

MY SCHOOL back in New York was a gray brick building in the middle of a city block. The nearest blade of grass was two blocks away in Central Park. But my new school, Dan Quayle Middle School, looked a lot like I imagined a typical American school would—a redbrick building on the outskirts of town, surrounded by three sports fields and a big digital scoreboard. Pretty impressive. On the first day of school, there was a green and white banner hanging over the main entrance that read WELCOME QUAILS!

The night before my first day, I was pacing around Pam's little house, pretending not to be nervous, when the phone rang.

It was Brett. "Stick close to me tomorrow," he said. "I'll smooth things out for you."

God looked down from the heavens and smiled on me. Truly I was one of the Chosen People. Without Brett, I would've taken my first terrified steps into that building alone only to be completely ignored. But with the quarterback by my side?

"Hey, come meet the Brain," he called out as he guided me down the main hall. "He's from New York! That's right, the Big Apple!"

I was in. The cool new kid. And you should've heard some of the questions.

Like: "Hey, New York. You ever been where John Lennon got shot?"

Or: "I hear you guys don't have any trees!"

Or: "How many times have you been mugged?"

I didn't care what they asked, I was just happy to have made it. The road was clear from here on out, because Brett was by my side.

First-period homeroom was in Room 421, a big room with blue walls and thirty desks, neatly arranged in rows. A poster on the far wall read HOOSIERS LOVE TO READ!

Walking in, I saw most of the kids I had invited to my bar mitzvah. Ryan and Eddie sitting together in the third row, laughing about something. Lucy and Kendra were whispering in a corner. Near the front, Nicole was joking around with J.D. and Seth. Bridget was leafing through a magazine near the back. Then Brett swooped in behind me and began introducing me to other people whose names I had been hearing over the past month. Just like in the halls, everyone seemed psyched to meet the new guy from New York. It was like I was a rock star for a day. This one kid started asking which Starbucks Tina Fey liked to go to and what she liked to drink. As if I knew. Luckily, Brett saved me.

"Over here, Brain," he said.

A minute later, I was at a desk at the back near Eddie and Ryan—a seat of honor, too, right next to the QB himself. No doubt about it: I was floating. All due respect to Steve and Bill, but back home I never hung out with a kid as cool as Brett. I took a long look around the room. Nice new friends, nice new school. Who'd have thought it? Maybe life in Appleton would work out after all.

"Yo, what is a bar matzah?"

Then again, maybe not.

I had been so busy lapping up my newfound coolness, I hadn't seen Fudge come in. But suddenly there he was, holding my bar mitzvah invitation by its edges like it was covered with armpit sweat. The mail in Appleton was fast, apparently.

"A party," I said, then quickly added, "It should be a blast."

Eddie wasn't so convinced. He grabbed Fudge's invite and narrowed his eyes.

"I got one of these on Saturday." He looked at me. "You mean it was from you?"

"Uh, yeah," I said, and pointed at Fudge's invite. "See my name? Evan Goldman."

Eddie looked mystified. "I thought your name was the Brain."

"Oh, check it out," Brett said. "I saw one of those fancy envelopes on our dining room table the other day."

I swallowed. "So you haven't opened it?"

Apparently not. Brett took Fudge's card and pointed to the last line.

"What is this stuff anyway?"

"That's Hebrew," I said, trying to sound cheerful.

Ryan looked concerned. "What's up with that? Are you an Arab or something?"

"No," Lucy said, walking over. "He's Jewish. My mom says this is some creepy Jewish thing where we all have to get baptized."

"It's not—it's just a party," I protested. I was starting to flush.

"Isn't this in like three weeks?" Brett was working hard to manipulate his mental calendar. "Because I've got football."

"No, I checked, there's no game that day," I

stammered. "It's just a party."

Fudge wrinkled his brow. "In the basement of a church?"

"Oh, come on, you'll have a great time!"

I felt like I was about to cry. After a grand entrance, I was suddenly like a week-old banana turning black in the fridge.

"Well, I gotta talk to my mom about this," Brett said, sounding dubious.

The teacher walked in. Mr. Hertz was a big fat redheaded guy with a huge mustache. "Okay, here we go!" he barked, and all the kids jumped into their chairs. I sat down hard in mine, thoroughly depressed. And things were about to get worse. Just after Mr. Hertz closed the door, it popped open and Patrice ran in.

"Sorry, sorry!"

I hadn't seen her in a week or so. She had clearly gotten dressed up for the first day of school and looked prettier than I had ever seen her. But as she skittered across the room to a desk next to the window, I heard Lucy and Kendra giggling. I knew, and Patrice knew, that they were laughing at her.

I tried not to look at Patrice too closely, but as Mr. Hertz took roll, I saw her eyes drift to Fudge's desk. As luck would have it, my invitation was sitting right there. Watching her read it, my stomach sank. The truth is that ever since I hadn't been able to drop her invite in the mailbox, I had felt torn. In a perfect world, Patrice would come to my party and have so much fun, she'd end up doing the hora with Lucy. But in real life, her presence would infuse the whole party with a giant chunk of weird. So even though I had half planned to mail her invite eventually, it was still at home on my desk.

Now she tried to catch my eye, but I turned away just in time and shouted "Here!" when I heard my name. It didn't matter, I reminded myself. Patrice wouldn't want to be at a party with all the cool kids anyway. Besides which, we weren't really even friends anymore.

Right?

• • •

Miraculously, the next two periods were both classes without Patrice. Brett was in English with me, Eddie was in everything with me, and the rest of the kids were around in various combinations. Now that the subject of my bar mitzvah had been broached, it seemed like everyone was basically pretending that it had never come up. I was desperate to ask people if they were going to come—Brett in particular—but I knew I had to ride it out a little.

The period before lunch, I was at my locker in the main hallway, alone for the first time all day. Then I realized that someone was standing behind me. I turned.

There was Patrice.

She was staring at me with a fierceness I had seen before only when she gave Lucy the evil eye.

I turned back to the locker. I fiddled with my lock. I waited.

But she didn't leave.

I turned to face her, expecting her to finally say something, but she just kept staring at me. There was so much going on in her face, I couldn't tell if she was sad or angry or happy to see me or just tired.

I tried to make things right. "Look, Patrice," I began. "I wanted to invite you. In fact, I have your invitation at home on my desk. Seriously."

Her face sort of crumpled in on itself. Her eyes got hard and sad. This wasn't going well.

"I just forgot to mail it," I said, panicking. "So I'll give it to you after school, all right?"

The irises of her eyes turned to ice. "You're a liar," she said. Suddenly she was crying. Then she was running away.

I called her name, but the bell rang, so I didn't know if she heard me or not. All right, I thought, if she wants to be dramatic about it, then fine. Sure I should've mailed her invitation, but I had done what I thought was right. Patrice would get over it. It wasn't that big a deal. After all, it was just a bar mitzvah. Everything was working out for the best.

Except.

The more I think about it, the more I think that betraying Patrice is what led to what happened next— like some Higher Power decided to balance the scales. As the second bell rang, I threw my backpack over my shoulder and started to run to lunch. If I hadn't had to tie my shoe, maybe it would have all happened differently. But no, right there, while I was on one knee rushing to get my laces tied, with no one else around, I heard the sound that would define my next few weeks.

DINK clump. DINK clump. DINK clump. DINK clump.

There he was. Archie, on crutches.

Our eyes met. I was surprised. I guess I had assumed that he went to a different school, one for kids with special needs.

"Hey," I said. "What's up?"

Archie smiled.

"So," he said. "I hear you're having a party."

ARCHIE DIDN'T sound like a normal person. First of all, he spoke very slowly, almost like he was stuttering. Then, when he finally did get a sentence out, his throat made this raspy, choking sound, and his voice bounced up and down, sometimes even within a single word. He didn't say "party"; he croaked "Pa" and then he squeaked "irrrr" and finally belched out "ty." Like everything else about Archie, it caught you off guard.

"Huh?" I said.

"You're having a party, right?" he repeated. Pa-irrrr-ty. "Everybody's talking about it."

He had a wide grin, and his eyes were set way off

to either side of his head, froglike, and he was a little pudgy. Sort of sweet looking, and with the crutches kind of defenseless, like a penguin. And the crutches weren't like the wooden ones that fit under your armpits like I used when I busted my foot skiing in fourth grade; these were heavy-duty aluminum things with cuffs for his arms to go through.

"Yeah," I said. "It's just a, um, bar mitzvah."

He leaned forward on his crutches. "I bet the city is really amazing. Is it like in the Storm Front episode when Silik and Archer go to Manhattan to stop Hitler and they end up resetting the Temporal Conduit?"

I felt bad about the crutches, but this guy was too weird for words. My eye caught the clock over his head. "Well, listen, it's been great talking to you, but I'm late for lunch."

"Oh, you'll be fine," Archie said. "Just tell them you were walking me to the nurse's office. You can always use me as an excuse. Whenever you don't want to do something or you get in trouble, just say, 'Sorry, I was helping out my friend who has muscular dystrophy.' Gets you off the hook every time."

I swallowed hard. "I appreciate that."

"And you don't even have to tell me," Archie went on. "I'll back you up. You're my friend."

I blinked. I was? We had only just met!

"Yeah," I stammered. "Okay. That's great." The

doors to all the classrooms along the hallway closed as class started. "I really have to get going."

If Archie heard, he didn't let on. He just clumped closer.

"Here's the thing," he said. "Since we're friends now, I was thinking that you should get me a date."

I looked around to see if anyone was playing a joke on me.

"With Kendra Peterson," he went on. "Can you make that happen?"

"I'm sorry?" I said.

Archie moved even closer. "You know, a date. Like to a movie. Or IHOP?"

"With Kendra?" I had to make sure I had heard right. "The head cheerleader? She's going out with Brett, the most popular boy in the whole school. You'll never get near her."

Archie rolled his eyes. "They're not *going out*. They haven't done the tongue."

"What does that mean?"

"That's the rule—you're not 'going out' until you do the tongue," Archie said. "And Kendra won't let Brett do it."

"I've never heard of this rule," I said skeptically.

"Well, I guess in New York City, you're all too busy being chased by muggers to worry about these things, but that's how it works out here."

"Listen, if she won't let Brett"—I felt ridiculous even saying it—"do the tongue with her, why would she let you?"

Clump, clump. He was standing as close to me as he could, his wild frog eyes glaring into mine. "I'm glad you asked." He turned to one side, then the other, checking to make sure no one could hear him. "This morning, in biology class?" He waited, building up the suspense. "I'm just sitting there, right? Being invisible, as always. And I look up, and Kendra's staring at me. So I'm like, whoa, what's that about? And before I could do anything . . ."

Silence. The sound of chalk writing on a blackboard in the classroom next to us. "What? Before you could do anything, what?"

Archie grinned—no, more like he beamed—and he said, "She smiled at me." He stepped back in triumph. He raised his eyebrows knowingly. "She likes me."

My head was starting to hurt.

Archie said, "So I was thinking that you could get me a date. I mean, you're new here and everyone likes you."

"That's because I haven't done anything stupid yet!" I said. More like yelled. This was getting a little bit scary. "One wrong move and I'm exiled to the Loser table for the rest of the year."

Archie wasn't listening.

"Or hey, wait a minute!" he said. "Maybe it'd be easier if I just sit next to her."

Now I was really confused. "When? At lunch?"

Archie shook his head. "No! At your bar mitzvah!"

I nearly fell over. Seriously. Flat on my face. Down for the count. Then Archie's face twisted into this sick sort of grin. "I can always just ask your mom if I can come."

See what I mean about the Higher Power punishing me for what I had done to Patrice?

"What?" I said.

Archie stared me down. "I mean, your mom's not gonna tell the little crippled kid he can't come to the party."

Suddenly there was nothing charming, quirky, or even sad about Archie. Disease or not, this was hardball. If he came to my bar mitzvah, I'd be doomed. Brett and his gang would never come!

"But here's the thing," he was saying. "This is a two-way deal. If you get me a date with Kendra, I'll do something for you. Get you and Patrice back together."

That pulled me up short.

"You're friends with Patrice?"

It was sort of hard to believe, considering she hadn't hung out with him all summer. At least, not since I'd arrived. Archie shrugged. "Oh, yeah, from way back before I got so sick. Also she feels sorry for me, so I take advantage of that. Like I said, I can get you two back together in no time."

"There's nothing to get back together," I said. "Patrice and I weren't really such great friends to begin with."

Archie didn't buy that for a second. "Oh, please," he said. "Until you met Brett and the rest of those idiots, I saw the two of you together practically every time I looked out the window." He leaned closer. "I can fix things. Patrice likes you." He leaned even closer. "I mean, she *likes* you."

I saw a teacher looking through the window of her classroom door. "Archie, can we talk about this later?"

"So you'll get me that date with Kendra? You will, right? You're gonna do it, right?"

By that point, Archie was so worked up that his chest started to heave a little bit and his leg shook. Then, behind me, someone spoke.

"Archie, are you all right? Do you need help getting to class?"

I turned to see a middle-aged woman with bright red hair and cat's-eye glasses standing at the other end of the hallway.

Archie transformed instantly. His eyes softened, his

posture loosened. He was suddenly a typical sweet twelve-year-old boy.

"That's okay, Mrs. Kincaid. Evan's helping me."

Mrs. Kincaid smiled. "Well, get a move on, you two. Evan, that's a very kind thing to do. Thank you."

I stammered, "Of course, Mrs. Kincaid."

As she walked off, she said, "Welcome to Appleton!"

The minute she was out of sight, Archie was grinning.

"You know what I could've done just then?" he said.

"What?"

He shrugged. "I could've flopped on the floor and told her you pushed me."

Did this kid have any limits? I must've gasped. Or turned white. Because suddenly Archie was giggling like a wild man.

"You should see yourself! Don't people joke around in New York? I wouldn't do that to you—you're my friend. You've got to relax."

"Okay," I choked. By that time I was leaning against a locker for support.

"But remember," Archie said, "good things can happen if you help me."

I was desperate to get away. Practically dying.

"Archie, listen. I've really got to go. We'll talk, okay?"

I began to walk away, fast. But ten feet or so down the hall, I heard a loud thud. When I turned there was Archie—on the floor, twitching and gasping like a freshly caught fish. Ten thousand thoughts rushed through my head at once. Had I done this to him somehow? Was he going to tell people I had pushed him? Was I his last-ever hope for happiness at that miserable school? Was he really in trouble?

"Hold on!" I cried. "I'll get the nurse!"

I was maybe ten steps down the hall when I realized that the gasping had stopped. I turned, expecting him to be dead, and instead he was propped up on his arms smiling impishly at me.

"Just imagine that on the dance floor in the middle of your bar mitzvah!"

"Archie!" I said.

His eyes narrowed. "Just get me that date!"

With that, Archie got himself up on his feet. It took forever. He couldn't just stand up. Instead, he had to brace his feet against the lockers, then walk forward on his hands until he was upright. Halfway through, I made a motion to help, but he stopped me with a glance.

"I've got it."

Once he was on his feet, he moved down the hall without another look. I was calculating in my head: What happens if I say yes? How do I get Kendra to go on a date with him? She's Brett's girlfriend! Or she will be soon. But what happens if I say no? If Archie tells my mother I didn't invite him, all of a sudden he's gonna be at the house every night eating dinner with us. And what if, oh my god, what if he really does come to the bar mitzvah and does the crazy fake seizure?

A little too quietly, I said, "I'll try."

Archie looked over his shoulder. "What?"

"I said I'll try, okay?"

You should've seen the grin the spread across his face—so hopeful. Like for the first time in years that someone had agreed to help him. I felt pretty good about myself, to tell the truth.

"I knew you would," he said, and sort of snorted.

And *DINK clump, DINK clump*, he was off down the hall.

IN NEW YORK, a bad day was a cab tearing through a puddle on a rainy day, dousing you with dirty water. Or getting stuck on the subway back from Shea after the Mets lost in the bottom of the ninth. Or having to spend the afternoon at Bloomingdale's shopping for pants with your mom. Annoying, but basically harmless. Apparently, a bad day in Indiana involved destroyed friendships and being threatened by the neighborhood psycho. After shaking loose of Archie, I ran to the cafeteria as fast as I could, but by the time I got there, they were just pulling up the food trays. I ran to the counter anyway, but the lady behind the cash register shooed me away.

"We stop serving at twelve thirty-five on the dot," she said.

I glanced at the clock. It was 12:37.

"What's a couple of minutes?" I said. "I need to eat."

The lady smiled. "And you can tomorrow. By twelve thirty-five."

Conversation over.

I turned and took in an entire lunchroom full of seventh graders throwing milk cartons, eating cookies, gossiping, and joking. I vaguely recognized some of the kids I had met earlier in the day, but Brett was nowhere to be seen, and neither were any of the other kids in his clique. I didn't know where to go.

Except there was Patrice, sitting by herself at a table near the door. And she was staring right at me. But then she turned away, buried her face in a notebook, and began to write furiously. I remembered seeing a whole stack of those notebooks on her bookshelf: her diaries, where she recorded every slight that had ever been directed at her in her twelve years of miserable existence on this earth. I didn't have to think too hard to wonder what she was writing about now.

Even so, I almost walked across the room and asked if I could join her. I felt just that weird and lonely. But then Archie clumped up, collapsed in the chair across from her, and took a bag lunch out of his knapsack. With nowhere else to go, I plopped down at a mostly empty table in the middle of the room, opened my own knapsack, and grabbed *Of Mice and Men*, the novel we had been assigned for English. Not that I had any desperate urge to get a head start on my work, but with no food and no friends, I had to do something to keep myself from shriveling into a depressed ball and blowing away. But even though the first few sentences were good, I just couldn't concentrate. I felt too hungry and alone to read. I riffled through the front pocket of my knapsack, grabbed my cell phone, even though they weren't allowed in school, and wrote a text to Steve:

HELP! I'm stuck in a universe of freaks! Call me!

But when I pressed send, the stupid thing wouldn't go through. Just as I was about to try again, I felt a strong grip on my shoulder.

"Hey, hey! You know the rules!"

Suddenly I was staring into the face of an insanely muscular bald guy. Clearly a phys ed teacher turned lunch monitor.

"The phone!" he said.

Argument was pointless. I handed it over.

"Pick it up tomorrow in the assistant principal's office with a note from home."

No phone. No way to contact my New York friends. No way to contact anyone! Totally depressed, I put my head down on my knapsack. Which is when I finally caught a break. That's because I felt something soft under my right temple. Curious, I looked inside the knapsack. Squashed underneath my new biology textbook was a brown bag.

My mom had packed lunch!

I turned it upside down over the table. Out spilled a turkey sandwich that looked like it had been run over by a truck, a small bag of baby carrots, and a box of raisins. Not much. But at least it was something. With the turkey smashed beyond recognition, I started in on the raisins and just sat there, waiting for the rest of the gang to show up. They didn't. And when I crumpled up my lunch bag to throw it away, I felt something else: an envelope with a note in my mom's squiggly handwriting.

To my brave young man on his first day of school. I am so proud of you. Love, Mom.

There were still ten minutes left to lunch. But there I was, sitting by myself in a giant cafeteria with an empty box of raisins, trying not to cry.

• • •

77

"About time you showed up, Brain!"

Fudge threw his shirt at me. The locker room smelled like feet.

"Where were you guys?" I asked. "I looked for you during lunch."

Eddie laughed. "You didn't actually go to the cafeteria?"

"Well, yeah," I said stupidly.

Fudge grinned. "Lunch is at the parking lot, Brain."

Brett poked his head around the corner. "Come on, you freaks! I want to get out there already!"

Fudge and Eddie pushed past me to get outside. I quickly changed, dumped my clothes in an empty locker, and ran behind them, up a ramp and onto the football field. I don't think I'd ever actually been on one—not one that was regulation size, anyway. It was the real deal, a hundred yards long. And curving around it was a track. Stenciled in the center of the field was the name of the football team: THE QUAYLE QUAILS.

By the time I got outside, Brett and the rest of the guys and girls were stretching. Next thing I knew, the gym teacher walked up. Guess who? The guy who took my cell phone. Just my luck. But if he recognized me, he didn't let on. Probably collected about fifty cell phones a day.

"All right!" he said. "The first few phys ed classes are going to be about working off some of that summer flab. Conditioning, my friends! So we'll start with laps. Slow and steady! I'm looking for endurance here! Get moving!"

I stood up. In New York, phys ed was kickball in the park. Was I really going to have to spend an entire period running? A minute later, we were going around the track. For half a lap, everything was cool. I took it light and easy. Endurance, after all. But then I felt a whack on the back of my head. Brett passed me, laughing.

"Pick it up, Brain! The girls are kicking your butt."

"But he said to take it slow!" I said.

Wrong answer.

Another whack on the head. This time Fudge cruised by, cracking up. I turned my head just in time to have Eddie slap me in the nose.

"Oh, dude, sorry!"

Brett turned back and yelled. "Come on, Brain! Move it!"

What happened to slow and steady? Ugh. I pumped harder, thinking of the cliff at the quarry. Was this another test?

We went around once. Twice. I'd almost catch up to Brett, but then he'd suddenly step on the gas and he'd be halfway around the track ahead of me. Fudge and Eddie were almost as fast. They'd slow down, then scamper off like a couple of rabbits, looking back and laughing.

Fine, jerks, I thought. I can do this.

I pushed hard off the balls of my feet and started driving forward as fast as I could. And amazingly, I began to catch up—even with the guys running full out. I passed Eddie first. Then Fudge. Then bam! I was right up to Brett! Wheezing, my eyes tearing from the wind, my heart pounding out of my chest, I lunged forward and passed him!

And he stuck his foot out and tripped me.

I flew off the track right into the Q of Quails and curled up in a ball with scraped knees and my hands pocked with gravel. I couldn't breathe.

"Is that Goldman?" That was the gym teacher "Get up, Goldman!" But I was immobile.

Then I felt something squeeze under my back. Suddenly I was in the air. Brett had picked me up.

"It's all right, Coach, I'll get him in to the nurse! Looks like he went down hard!"

I saw the gym teacher give Brett a thumbs-up.

"Good man, Connelly!"

• • •

I walked stiffly down the hall, with Brett supporting me.

"What was that about?" I asked. "You didn't have to trip me!"

Brett seemed to be keeping himself from laughing.

"I didn't trip you, Brain. You were just running too hard out there. You gotta learn to take it easy."

My body hurt. I didn't want to have to explain this all to the nurse, either. It was my first day!

"This way, dude."

Brett pushed open a door and guided me inside. But it wasn't the nurse's office, just an empty classroom, one of the science labs.

"What are we doing in here?"

Brett checked to make sure nobody was in the room, then grabbed a chair and propped it against the door so no one could get in.

"Gotta talk to you, Brain."

"Wait a second," I said. "Aren't we going to the nurse?"

Brett smiled. Suddenly he was back to being the likable guy I had met at Calvi's a few weeks earlier. "You don't need a nurse. I got us out of gym because I need you to help me out."

I have to say that I was pretty surprised. One minute the guy is taunting me, the next he's asking for help? Besides, how could I, the new kid in town, help the Savior of Indiana?

Brett pulled a chair next to mine. "You're gonna need to get us into the movies on Friday night."

I blinked. "What?"

"*The Bloodmaster*, dude. We all wanna go see it on Friday at the mall, but it's rated R."

This was the horror flick Brett, Eddie, and Fudge had been talking about on the way to the quarry.

"That's it? That's all you need me to do?" I asked.

Brett nodded. I took a deep breath and smiled for the first time in hours. Finally some good news. This was going to be easy.

"There's six other movies in that mall," I said. "Just say you're going to a different one. I do it all the time in New York."

Brett shook his head. "Too bad this isn't New York." He stood up and leaned against the blackboard. "They won't let you in unless a grown-up buys the tickets, then goes in with you. They've got security watching."

I shrugged. Still seemed easy enough to me. "Then just get your mom to go."

Brett raised his eyebrows. "I don't think she's gonna blow off the Crusade for Christ so we can all see *The Bloodmaster*." He paused. Again came the golden grin. "Besides which . . . if my mom was there, that would ruin my plan."

This was getting complicated. "What plan?"

Brett shrugged. "Keep your trap shut, Brain, but Friday night, I'm going to make Kendra my girl."

It had been a long day. It seemed like ages since

homeroom. But I still remembered what Archie had said about the Indiana rules.

"You mean you're going to . . ."

Brett smiled, then tilted back his head and wagged his tongue to the heavens.

"Tongue time!" he said.

I thought briefly of Nina Handleman—how I had been content enough with her top lip.

"Wow," I said, smiling. "Yeah, I guess you wouldn't want your mom around for that."

Brett was all business again. "Exactly. So your mom'll have to come."

My mom? Could I tell Brett I hadn't talked to her in two weeks?

"Wow, Brett, I don't know." I sighed. "She gets wigged out if she cuts herself shaving her legs. She's not big on horror movies."

Brett shook his head. "You're not thinking of this the right way, Brain. Picture it! Kendra sitting next to me. Girl on screen being eaten by monster. Kendra burying her head in my chest. Me comforting Kendra. Kendra looking up lovingly. Me stuffing my tongue down her throat." Brett looked at me. "You don't want to stand in the way of something that beautiful."

Didn't sound too romantic to me. Then again, if it were me and the girl was Nina, well, I might think differently. I stood up. By that point, I realized what was expected—another twist in a completely insane day.

"I can try, man," I said.

Brett was moving to the door. "No, no. Don't just try, Brain. Get it right, okay?"

"Okay," I said. Then I shrugged. "But what if she says no?"

Brett opened the door. "Simple. If she says no, you make her say yes. Or else I'm not coming to your little bits mits—" He paused and searched for the word. "Your biz mizz—" He paused again. This time an arm went out as though he were trying to grab the words out of the air. Finally he just turned to me and looked right in my eyes. "Make it work or none of us are coming to your little party."

The door slammed and I was alone with the test tubes.

I PEEKED outside the door, checking for any hall monitors who might catch me wandering around school in the middle of sixth period in my gym clothes. Coast was clear. I stepped out.

DINK clump.

"It's perfect. You don't even know it's perfect, but it's soooo perfect."

Archie had been listening outside the door the whole time, apparently.

I sighed. "Listen, I don't want to get in any trouble, okay? I just want to get back to the locker room and change my clothes, and then I want to go to last period and then I want to crawl into a hole and die."

He shook his head. "No, no, no! You're missing the point! I know you're all nervous about the movie, and what if they don't come to your party, and whatever, but look! This is not a catastrophe—this is an opportunity!"

It had been a ridiculously long day.

"Come on," Archie went on. "I'll walk you to the gym. That way nobody will give you trouble."

All right, score one for the kid with the disease. "Okay," I said. "I'm listening. Why is this such an opportunity?"

Archie handed me his book bag and smiled as he took my arm. "Because you get to solve two problems at the same time!"

"I don't understand."

"It's perfect," Archie continued. "You get to be a big hero by getting all the kids into the movie. And I get to come and sit next to Kendra!"

I stopped short. "Wait a second! You're coming to the movie too?"

Archie kept right on moving, even faster than before. I had to hurry to catch up. "Of course I'm coming to the movie!" he said. "That's how I'm going to steal Kendra away from Brett!"

"But wait—"

"It'll be easy!" he said. "She'll end up giving *me* the tongue. Not the dumb jock."

At this point I just gave up fighting. Okay, I thought, if Archie wants to live in Fantasyland, then let him. He can come to the movie and make an ass of himself and all I have to do is let it happen. At least then I can say that I did my part to get him near Kendra, and he won't crash my bar mitzvah.

"You're right, Archie," I said. "If I can make this work, it'll be awesome. But help me out here. How am I supposed to get my mom to buy six tickets to a horror movie on Friday night?"

"You could tell her your life depends on it?" Archie said.

That's when Patrice walked by. You could tell by the look on her face that she wanted to avoid me just as much as I wanted to avoid her. But with everyone in class, the halls were pretty much empty. And I'd like to say that we patched things up right on the spot. I'd like to say that I apologized, sincerely and completely, and Patrice graciously acknowledged that she had been responsible as well. Instead, things got worse.

"Hey, Patrice!" Archie said. "You'll never guess! Evan's going to get me a date with Kendra!"

Patrice looked like she had just taken a bite out of a piece of roadkill.

"He what?" she said to Archie. I guess she was so stunned, she actually talked to me. "You what?"

"I said I'd *try*, Archie! That's all."

But Archie wasn't listening. He was on a roll. "We're all going to *The Bloodmaster* Friday night."

To my surprise, Patrice laughed. "This I gotta see."

Was she really going to be such an annoying nag? Didn't she understand the pressure I was under?

"Good luck," I said. "*The Bloodmaster*'s rated R. You won't get in."

Patrice's face hardened. She wasn't nearly as cute when she was mad at me. "Oh, don't worry," she said. "I'll get in."

"Fine!" I said.

She said it back. More like yelled it. "Fine!"

With that, she stomped down the hall away from me, the second time in one day.

"Don't worry, Evan," Archie said. "She wants you."

I resisted the urge to punch him. "What I'm worried about is getting my mother to buy these tickets."

Archie laughed. "Piece of cake."

"For one thing, we have no money. For another, she'd rather poke out her eyeballs with a fork than sit through *The Bloodmaster*. And on top of everything, I haven't even spoken to her in two weeks!"

Archie smiled broadly, cheerfully. He giggled. He snorted.

"What? What's so funny?"

"Don't you have some sort of magic Jewish power

to make people do something they don't want to do?"

And like a flash, it hit me. I DO have a magic Jewish power: the power of . . . guilt!

• • •

I've heard people of all religions say they know about guilt, but I think Jews really do have the corner on this particular art form. Jewish guilt is not something you can teach, it's not even something you can define, but perhaps I can offer you this opportunity to study it.

There are three components to Classic Jewish Guilt.

1. Don't worry about me, I'm fine.
2. You didn't do anything wrong, it was really my fault.
3. You couldn't really fix it anyway, you're far too busy. I'll take care of it.

Now watch as I deploy those elements. I may be young, but I've got a real gift for this. It is a gift given to me by ten thousand years of suffering.

• • •

It is late afternoon. The bus has dropped me off at Pam's house. I enter with my book bag. I look exhausted. Pam and my mother are drinking coffee at the kitchen table.

"Hey, tiger!" Pam says.

I sigh.

My mother says, "How was your first day of school?"

I haven't really spoken to my mother in two weeks, so she is surprised when I say, "I think it'll be okay, really."

Pam laughs. "Well, that doesn't sound too enthusiastic."

I sigh again, then say, "I think I'm going to lie down for a while."

I carry my book bag into my room as though I've been walking through the Sinai Desert. I lie down on my bed.

Shortly thereafter, a knock. My mother peeks her head in the door.

"You okay, kiddo?"

I sit up on my elbows. My mother enters, sits on the bed next to me.

"Sure, Mom. I'm just adjusting."

A meaningful pause.

I clear my throat. "You know, Mom, I realized today that I've been unfair."

My mother looks surprised. "What do you mean?"

"I know this isn't your fault," I say. "I know you've had to make a lot of really difficult choices and you're doing the best you can. And I really respect you for the way you're handling things."

My mother blushes. A tear comes to her eye. "Oh, honey, I don't actually think I'm doing all that well by you."

"No," I say emphatically. "You are. You've been so strong and I've been . . . I've been mean, Mom. I'm sorry."

She hugs me. "Thank you, Evan."

"You know," I go on, "I just think that kids have to go through trials. That's how we grow. Something tough happens and we just push through."

She wipes her eyes. "Sure."

"I have to learn to be strong. As strong as you've been."

She's starting to look a little guilty. I'm doing very well.

"So when Friday night comes, instead of hanging out with the rest of the gang and going to the coolest movie of the year, I'll stay here with you and Pam." I pause. "And practice my haftorah."

A quizzical look. "What movie?"

"Oh, it doesn't matter." I pull my notebook out of my book bag and set it on the desk. "The point is I don't really need *friends*. Look, I would love more than anything to find a way to get everyone in to see it, but I can't because it's R-rated and their parents won't let them. Besides, I've got all I need right here in this tiny windowless bedroom. What I need is faith in myself. Like you have."

I begin doing my math homework.

"Wait a minute, Evan, I never said you don't need friends."

Here's the key moment: I DON'T LOOK AT HER.

(A note: The temptation here is to turn, look really excited, and beg her to let you go. But you have to hold on, because it's about to get even better.)

"Oh, Mom," I say, sharpening a pencil, "it's all right."

She kneels down and looks me in the eye. "Evan Goldman, you stop being silly. Tell you what. If your new friends have parents who won't take them to see some stupid R-rated movie, then I suppose we'll just have to take matters into our own hands."

"Oh?" I say.

Mom takes my hand. "We'll make sure everyone gets into the movie, easiest thing in the world. Then I'll get lost—like I wasn't even there, okay?"

The smile has to be carefully chosen here. You cannot smile triumphantly; you must smile with simple, radiant gratitude.

"Do you mean it, Mom? After all I've put you through, you would do that for me?"

She kisses me on the cheek. "Do your homework, kiddo. Dinner's in an hour." She turns to go. She opens the door.

Wait for it. Wait for it.

"In fact," she says, "I'll even buy the tickets!"

• • •

And that is how we all got to *The Bloodmaster* on Friday night.

ON FRIDAY Mom really came through. She drove me to the mall, nodded "Hi" to Brett and the kids, marched up to the ticket booth, and bought seven tickets—her treat, just like she had promised, then walked us into the theater.

"Have fun!"

With a quick wave, she turned back to her car.

You should've seen it. I was high-fived, back-slapped, and congratulated like I had just completed a solo climb up Everest. I had done it! Made everything right! Now everyone would come to my bar mitzvah. When Brett threw his arm around my shoulder, I felt almost giddy.

"Whoa, Brain," he said. "Your mom rules!"

"Thanks, Brett buddy."

Moments later, Brett, Eddie, Fudge, and I were loaded down with popcorn, soda, and candy, while Kendra and Lucy took a sprint to the bathroom.

"Yo, Brett!" Eddie said. "Front two rows are open!"

As it turned out, every row was open. I guess *The Bloodmaster* wasn't high on most people's must-see list. The place was empty.

"Come on!" Fudge said, and marched down the aisle.

Things were going well, right? But it turned out I was in for my own private horror movie that night. The minute my butt hit my seat, I heard her.

"Hey, Evan."

I had never really believed that Patrice would bother to come. And if she *did* decide to come, I didn't think she'd get in. But there she was, suddenly in the seat right behind me, with a copy of *The Hours*.

"Oh," I said. "You got in, I guess."

"My cousin works concessions," she said. "He snuck us in the emergency exit."

"Us?" I said, turning.

Patrice was half smiling, like she couldn't wait to

95

see my expertly planned evening get blown to bits.

"That's right," Patrice said. "Archie figured it was easier than trying to convince his mom to walk us in."

I had hoped that Archie would just chicken out. He had spent the last two days on my case morning, noon, and night, asking me what to wear, what to say, how to act. It was like I was suddenly his personal life coach. The night before, he had dropped by Pam's house unannounced.

"Yeah?" I said, when I opened the door.

Archie didn't waste any time. "I imagine you've noticed that I have a very powerful, very masculine smell."

I just stared at him sort of blankly.

"Even so," he went on. "I think my natural musk should be highlighted with cologne. What do you prefer? Brut or Old Spice?"

I was so weirded out that I mumbled something about homework and shut the door in his face. Did that stop Archie? Not even close. Later that night as I was struggling to learn my haftorah, he called.

"I've been making out with my pillow!"

I nearly dropped the phone. "You what?"

"You know, pretending it's Kendra. For when I plant the tongue later. Can you give me a few tips?"

"Oh, my god!" I shrieked, and hung up.

Thankfully, I hadn't seen or heard from him since. In my heart, I hoped he would realize how silly he sounded. I hoped he would give up on his dreams about Kendra. I hoped he would let me off the hook. I had even gotten Steve on the phone back in New York and asked his advice about what to do in case Archie showed up. "Do?" Steve had said. "If this Archie kid is as weird as you say, pretend you don't know him."

Which is what I wanted to do when I turned to see Archie clomping down the aisle, wearing the most outrageous getup I had ever seen in my life. I had told Archie to wear something casual, nothing too fancy. Instead, there he was, head to toe in this wild purple suit. I don't mean that just *some* of it was purple, I mean that *everything* was purple: his jacket, shirt, pants—even his socks—like he was a member of some psychedelic rock band.

"Hey!" he shouted. Then louder: "Hey! Hey!"

The nightmare had begun. Now that Archie was here, I had to stave off disaster. So I jumped out of my seat, dragged Archie back up the aisle, and got him to a dark corner of the lobby.

"What are you wearing?" I yelped. "Everyone's gonna make fun of you!"

Archie ignored that completely.

"I'm ready," he said. "Let me at her!"

I swear, he was practically panting.

"Okay, listen, here's the plan," I said. "You stay in the lobby until the right time."

Archie looked confused. "The right time? How am I going to know the right time?"

I thought fast. "I'll come and get you after the movie's been going a little while. I'm going to make sure I'm sitting next to Kendra. Then you come in and take my seat."

Archie smiled. "So that's when I slip her the tongue, right?"

"No," I said. "No tongue! Forget the tongue!"

I could not believe that a boy who looked like Barney the Dinosaur thought he was the George Clooney of Indiana.

Archie looked taken aback. "No tongue?"

"Just talk to her, okay? Say 'Hi, Kendra,' and then take it from there."

To that, Archie winked. "Relax. The love guru has everything under control."

"Love guru?" I said.

Archie nodded. "I'll have Kendra eating out of my hand by the Bloodmaster's first killing. Watch and learn."

"Okay, whatever," I said, trying not to get sucked into a ridiculous discussion. Still, I had to cover my tracks. I couldn't let Brett and the gang know I knew that Archie might crash the movie. "Just remember: You've got to pretend you didn't know any of us were here. You just happened to wander into the same movie."

"Yeah, yeah," Archie said. "Whatever you say."

"Fine," I said. "Just stay here and wait for my signal."

As I reentered the theater, the credits were rolling, so I hustled down the aisle. By the time I reached the front row, Kendra and Lucy had already come back from the ladies' room, and Kendra was sitting next to Brett with an empty seat on her other side. Maybe the Higher Power wanted Archie to get his shot at Kendra after all.

"Have a seat, Evan," Kendra said.

She patted the empty chair.

"Righto," Brett said. "The Brain's gotta be in the front row."

I breathed a sigh of relief. This could work out after all.

Seated behind Brett was Fudge. Lucy was next to him. From the way she was pouting, you didn't need to be a genius to see how badly she wanted to be next to Brett.

And then there was Patrice, still a row back, now next to Fudge with an empty seat between them, which made the first two rows look like this:

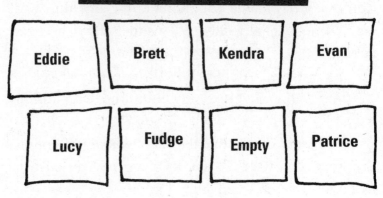

"Hey, Evan," Patrice said.

"What?"

"Where's your friend?"

"What friend?" Brett asked.

Thankfully, I was saved.

"Yo, yo!" Eddie called. He pointed to the screen. "Check this out!"

The screen filled with the image of a quaint Midwestern house, not unlike Pam's. *The Bloodmaster* was the story of this girl named Jessica Jones. In the first sequence she has a fight with her mom and dad, then gets stood up at the junior prom. But worse is yet to come. About five minutes into the film, she's walking down this deserted street and hears footsteps. She starts to run. The music gets loud. And you'll never guess who's behind her with a pickax. Next thing, the ax is implanted in her skull and the Bloodmaster, this tall guy with a hood over his head, is eating her arm. Fudge, Lucy, and Eddie screamed. Kendra called, "I can't watch this!" On-screen the Bloodmaster finishes his meal and burps really loudly. That's when Brett weighed in.

"Oh, man! Gross!"

"Hey, Ken," Lucy called. "This movie's going to be pretty intense from the very front row. I'd be happy to switch seats."

By that point, Brett had his arm around Kendra. She glanced back. "That's okay, Lucy. I'm fine."

It was obvious to everyone that Lucy liked Brett, but that didn't slow Fudge down. He put his arm around Lucy the minute Kendra turned back to the screen.

"May I interest you in some Goobers, Lucy?" he asked.

She scowled and pushed him away, then leaned forward to Eddie, sitting on the other side of Brett.

"All right, barf bag. Give up your seat."

"Like hell," Eddie said.

Lucy's response was simple. She took her soda and dumped it in Eddie's lap.

"Oh, I'm so sorry!" she called, as Eddie jumped up. "You better get cleaned up in the bathroom. 'Bye!"

"This sucks!" Eddie said, and hustled up the aisle, brushing off his pants.

Lucy jumped right into his seat and leaned in to Brett. "The view is so much better from here."

Now the seating looked like this:

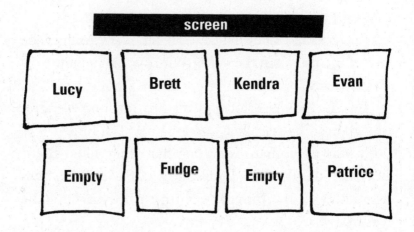

So there we were. I was settling in, watching the Bloodmaster pick his teeth with his bloody pickax, when I heard the scariest noise in the world.

DINK clump.

DINK clump.

"Oh, what a long walk! Down this long aisle! With these big crutches!"

Had Archie waited for me? Of course not!

"Oh, I'm so very tired," he went on. "I wonder if anyone will give me their seat."

I had no choice.

"Hey, man," I said, getting up. "Why don't you take mine? You must be exhausted."

I jumped into the second row next to Patrice and held my breath. Despite the gore on-screen, I was more scared of what was about to happen off it. No tongue, I thought, please please please no tongue.

Thankfully, he didn't. Even better, as Archie sat down, Kendra turned to him with a big smile and introduced herself.

"Hi. I'm Kendra."

Here it was: Archie's golden opportunity. Go on, I thought. Talk to her! Do it! Do it!

But if Archie had any words, he was suddenly too wound up to say them. The swagger he had shown in the lobby was gone. The love guru was suddenly sweating and hyperventilating.

"Are you all right?" Kendra asked.

Archie couldn't answer—just kept on breathing, louder and louder.

"Okay," she said. "Whatever."

"Great job," Patrice whispered to me.

"He just needs a second," I said. "Back off."

That's when he finally took my advice.

"HI, KENDRA!" he screamed at the top of his lungs.

Kendra looked at him like he was a mental patient.

"Yo, dude!" Brett said. "Keep it down!"

Brett might have done more—like picked him up and moved him to another part of the theater—but Archie was saved from complete and total humiliation by what was happening on-screen. Right then, Jessica's brother Clyde was confiding in the school principal. Unfortunately, the principal was actually the Bloodmaster. Just as Clyde was beginning to weep over his chopped-up sister, out came the pickax. This time the Bloodmaster didn't settle for chowing on an arm. Instead, he went straight for Clyde's head. Everyone in the movie theater moaned—especially when the Bloodmaster spit a mouthful of brains directly at the screen.

The drama in the audience was just as intense. After the Bloodmaster spit those brains, Eddie got back from the bathroom and sat next to Fudge in the second row. Now the seating was this:

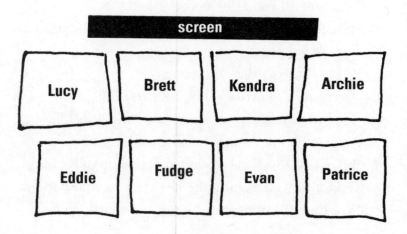

"Yo!" Eddie called. "Who's the weirdo with the stupid suit?"

Did Archie take it in stride? Not a chance. Suddenly he got into defending his crazy purple suit like it was a sacred artifact.

"It's not a STUPID SUIT!" he called, turning around in his seat. "It's a lucky suit, it's not STUPID!"

While Brett, Lucy, Fudge, and Eddie were looking at Archie like he was something that had crawled from out of an Egyptian tomb, Kendra tried to make him feel better.

"Hey, it's not a stupid suit," she said. "He didn't mean it."

Well, that was all the encouragement Archie needed. Eyes wide, he leaned right in to her.

"HI, KENDRA! HI! HI!"

He was so loud, you could barely hear the Bloodmaster belching.

It was bad enough that I couldn't watch the movie; now I couldn't even watch the audience.

Fudge suddenly lost it. Maybe he was trying to impress Lucy with his bravado, but for whatever reason, he started smacking Archie on the back of the head.

"Hey, cripple," he said. "Why don't you get out of here? Stop ruining the movie!"

Brett looked over his shoulder and punched Fudge

on the leg. "Yo, that's pretty harsh, Fudgeman."

But Fudge was on a roll, and not even Brett could stop him. "No, I mean it!" he said, standing up. "Get lost, cripple! Get out of here!"

Then Eddie got in the act.

"He can't," he said, giggling. "He's too busy putting the moves on Kendra!"

Lucy laughed.

"The cripple's getting some action!" Eddie yelled.

The totally confident Archie from the lobby had disappeared. Instead, he shook his head, pushed himself up on his feet, then flailed around in the dark for his crutches.

"Don't worry," he said. "I'm going!"

Seconds later he was clomping pathetically up the aisle. I was stunned. But the catastrophe wasn't over.

Patrice turned to me. "Are you just going to sit there?"

She climbed out of her seat and ran after Archie.

I remember that my third-grade teacher, Mr. Horowitz, once said that the secret of a life well lived is to take the right action at the right time. I don't know if that's true or not. But if it is, I failed. A side of me wanted to defend Archie. But the other side of me felt he deserved everything he got. Sure, Fudge shouldn't have said what he said. On the other hand, what right did Archie have to crash the party and ruin the movie? What right did he have to coerce me into helping him in the first place?

I watched Archie and Patrice disappear up the aisle while Fudge and Eddie snickered.

"You didn't have to be so mean, Fudge," I said finally.

I don't know if he even heard me. Just then, Kendra pointed at the screen, and Archie was forgotten.

"Brett! She's got a knife!"

"I've got you, Kendra," Brett said, pulling her closer. "I'm here."

I turned to the screen. While I had been focused on Archie, things had been heating up in the movie. Like Kendra had said, Jessica's mom had a knife. The Bloodmaster was begging for his life in his office. But then the Bloodmaster knocked the knife out of her hand and started munching her leg. Jessica's mother screamed. We all screamed. But no one louder than Lucy, because that's when Brett decided to make his move. He pulled Kendra's face up to his and moved in for the kiss.

Hands clasping hands. Eyes staring into eyes. One tongue reaching out to another. . . .

Just when their lips were about to touch—and as the Bloodmaster moved to Jessica's mom's second leg—the movie stopped.

The lights went on.

Next thing I knew, Patrice was running back down the aisle.

"Guys!" she said. "You'd better go! The manager stopped the movie, and he's about to call your parents!"

Kendra was up on her feet. "Call our parents? Why?"

"Well," Patrice said, glancing vaguely up the aisle, "I guess that *someone* told the manager that there were some underage people in here."

Then I saw Archie moving slowly back down the aisle, a self-satisfied smirk on his face.

"And maybe," Patrice went on, "that person gave him all your names."

"Archie!" I said.

Then Fudge climbed over the front-row seats and was in Archie's face.

"What's up with that? Why'd you have to bust us?"

Eddie joined him. "The cripple did it?"

Archie met his eyes with a cold stare. "Yeah. The cripple did it."

"Why, dude?" Brett asked. "We were just watching a movie!"

Archie shrugged. "Ask Evan. He's the one who invited me."

I've never been in quicksand, but I suddenly had a good idea of how it felt. "What?" I shouted. "No, I didn't!" I turned to Brett. "He invited himself!"

Archie shook his head. "No, no! We worked it all out so I could take his seat."

"But I was just—"

Brett didn't let me finish. Suddenly everything was my fault.

"The movie's ruined!" he barked. "We're all going to be friggin' destroyed by our parents!" He stood an inch away. "And my *tongue* is still waiting."

I was sinking fast.

"I didn't know any of this was going to happen," I said.

Then Fudge piped up. "I know something that'll cheer you up, Brett."

Brett smiled. "You don't mean—?"

Grinning, Fudge replied, "I do!"

Then Brett, Eddie, and Fudge shouted in perfect unison: "The triple hammer crack-splitting wedgie!"

Do I have to tell you what came next? I think I heard Kendra object, but Fudge and Eddie grabbed my arms anyway while Brett came around my back. He pulled so hard on my underwear, he practically lifted me off my feet. I could feel it ripping all the way up my butt crack, then shredding altogether.

I fell to the ground, my eyes watering. My throat

squeaked out the words "Does this mean you're not coming to my bar mitzvah?"

They didn't answer—they just scrammed out the emergency exit before the manager could get them. By now the theater was completely empty. Except for Archie and Patrice. They moved in for the final kill.

"You didn't do anything!" Archie yelled. "They called me a cripple and you didn't even help!"

"How could you just sit there and watch that happen?" Patrice said. "Don't you have a soul?"

Pretty harsh words to a guy who just had his underwear taken off over his head.

"Listen," I said, rising to my knees. "He wanted a date. He got a date!" I turned to Archie. "If you had just talked to her!"

But Archie wasn't listening. "You wanted to get rid of me!" he said. "You wanted to humiliate me!"

"What happened to thank you?" I said. "'Thank you, Evan, for getting me a chance with Kendra. Thank you for getting your ass kicked for doing me a favor!'"

Let's just say Archie and Patrice didn't see the situation my way. "Come on, Archie," Patrice said. "My dad'll give us a ride."

They turned toward the exit.

"Hey, wait," I called after them. "Are you just

going to abandon me here?"

Patrice looked back at me, the sadness in her eyes mingling with the anger. "Now you know how it feels."

AFTER PATRICE and Archie left, I lurked around the theater lobby for a full hour before Pam came to get me. Meanwhile I pieced together what happened with the rest of the gang:

> 1. *Brett and Kendra had a huge fight in front of the theater where she blamed the whole disaster on him and called him a "dumb jock."*
> 2. *Lucy offered to give Brett a ride home and sidled next to him in the backseat of her mom's car.*
> 3. *Fudge and Eddie made a vow to punish me even more severely on Monday at school.*

Sunday morning I had another haftorah lesson. As you can imagine, I wasn't in the holiest of moods. For starters, I still had a phantom pain where my underwear had cut up my butt. Second, how could I focus on Hebrew when all I could think about was what was going to happen to me at school on Monday?

"*Koh-amar ha'el Adoshem. Boray Hashamayim venoteyhem.*"

That was the rabbi, chanting the beginning of the lesson. I tried to repeat it.

"*Boray Hashammm . . .*"

"No, no, Evan," he said. He pulled up a chair next to me. "Listen again. *Koh-amar ha'el Adoshem. Boray Hashamayim venoteyhem.*"

The words stuck in my throat. When I finally said them, they came out more Swahili than Hebrew. The rabbi tapped my textbook with his index finger and smiled. "Your bar mitzvah is two weeks away. Try harder, Evan."

I'm not embarrassed to say that by that point, I was blinking back a tear or two. Call it genuine depression or pathetic self-pity, but I was feeling low big-time.

"Try harder?" I managed. "I've tried as hard as I can."

The rabbi shrugged and picked a small piece of lint off of his pant leg. "You know, Evan, no one said becoming a man was easy."

"I didn't ask for easy," I said. "This just isn't fair."

He sighed. "Growing up isn't always fun, you know."

"All I want is to fit in with the people who fit in." My eyes went back to the Hebrew, but he leaned over and closed the book.

"Seriously, Evan," he said. "Tell me. What's so important about being popular?"

I was floored. How could the only rabbi in Indiana not know what it felt like to be an outcast? The horrible feeling of eating your lunch all alone? Being the only kid not invited to a party? Didn't he know what it meant to be cool? That you always had a crowd? That you were a somebody who was a part of something?

"All right, listen," he said, turning to face me. "One day, you're going to be old. You don't believe that right now, but it's true. And when you're old, all of this . . . *mishegoss* about being 'cool' and being 'popular' will be a million miles away."

So what? I thought. I've got to deal with it now! I opened my mouth to say something, but the rabbi put up his hand.

"You're going to have children, Evan, you're going to have a job, you're going to have lots of important things to worry about. This is not one of them."

Conversation over, I thought. I reached for my books. But just like that the rabbi had a thick arm around my shoulder. He pulled me close and looked me straight in the eye.

"Be a man, Evan."

And for the first time in my life, I wanted to.

• • •

Be a man. How would a man handle this situation? I spent that afternoon spread-eagle on my bed in a stupor, thinking some more about what would happen at school at Monday.

Suddenly it hit me. This is what my speech should be about! I grabbed the paper and pen and wrote:

Manhood, by Evan David Goldman

According to Hebrew law and tradition, today is the day I become a man. Unfortunately, I don't know anything about what that means. I looked in the dictionary, and it talked about "courage," and "determination," and "vigor."

But what is the meaning of courage?

After that, I got stuck. Which turned out to be excellent timing, because Mom was at the door.

"Evan."

"Hold on, Mom," I said. "I'm writing the speech!"

Then I saw that she was holding the cordless.

"Evan," she said. "It's your father."

The daily call. And even though I really needed someone to talk to, my first impulse was to keep up the silent treatment.

"Tell him I'm busy."

Usually Mom was all too happy to pass along a message like that. But this day was different. She put her hand over the receiver.

"Why not just say hi?"

I blinked.

"Really?"

"Oh, Evan . . ." Her voice trailed off, then she went on, half to herself. "You can't stay angry forever."

I wasn't so sure about that. But what could I do? Suddenly, the phone was in my hand. Dad was on the line. Mom was looking on. Forces larger than myself were conspiring to make me take the call. Besides, deep down I wanted to speak to him. I'd wanted to for weeks. Slowly I drew the receiver up to my ear, then I paused a minute, just sort of listening to Dad breathe, getting a sense of him.

"Hello?" I said finally.

"Hey, Evan, buddy."

I felt my throat get tight and waved Mom out of the room.

"Hey," I said.

"It's good to hear your voice."

I made a sound in response, though I can't really say whether it was an actual word. Dad took that as a cue to go on. He laughed sort of awkwardly.

"I guess you've been pretty mad at me."

How could I answer that? With my eyes moist, it was hard to feel angry.

"Well," I began.

"No, it's okay," Dad said. "I understand where you're coming from. I guess I could tell you all day long that I never meant to hurt you or your mother and you'd still be mad and I wouldn't blame you. What's important is that I miss you a ton, big guy. I love you. Always will."

Apparently I had two months of tears hiding behind my face, just waiting for my dad. Suddenly I was full-fledged snot-out-of-the-nose bawling. And not only because my father had told me he missed and loved me. No, I was crying over everything: how hard it had been since we moved, how much I missed New York, how stupid I had been with Patrice, and the disaster of *The Bloodmaster*.

And as soon as I had control of my tear ducts enough to talk, I really let Dad have it. Maybe it wasn't fair. I mean, who knew why he fell for Angelina? Maybe he really had found true love.

Maybe my mom was a lousy wife. But at that moment I didn't care. Suddenly I was yelling, blaming him for everything rotten in my lousy life.

And I had to give my dad some credit. He didn't hang up. He didn't try to cut me off. He just took it. Only when I had screamed myself out to the point of being a quivering wreck, twitching on my bed, did Dad finally respond. Then he said all the right things. First, that he was sorry for everything. Then he told me again how much he loved me. And then came the capper.

He invited me to come out the following weekend.

"We can see a game," he said. "It's been too long, hasn't it?"

It had. And in the back of my mind was Aaron Siegel's bar mitzvah. It would be great to see everyone.

"But wait," I said. "What about Mom?"

"What about her?"

"She won't like it."

He chuckled. "I already cleared it with her, champ. She's probably printing out the tickets right now."

I was so happy that I ran out and gave my mother an actual hug—maybe the first since we had moved. Then I hurried to the living room to type a group e-mail to my New York gang.

Spread the word! Coming home for the weekend!

Then I dashed off another to Aaron Siegel, making sure it was still all right to come to his bar mitzvah.

Too excited to stay put, I grabbed Simon and took him out for a run around town. The "Evan moves back to New York" scenarios came fast and furious. Number one had to do with Angelina contracting rabies from a bad squirrel bite and being institutionalized, and Mom and me moving back. In number two, Nina Handelman invited me to move in with her to our own private love nest.

So what if I was hanging my hopes a little bit high? After all, it was only one stupid weekend. Deep down, I knew nothing permanent would come of it. Still, at that point a trip east seemed like the best thing that had happened to me since . . . well, since I had grazed Nina's upper lip.

WALKING TO school that Monday, I expected to be teased, put down, and otherwise insulted halfway into the twenty-second century. Who knew what horrible punishment Eddie and Fudge had come up with over the weekend? All I knew was that whatever they had in store was certain to be terrible.

And it was—only not in the way I pictured it. There were no more wedgies, no more insults. It was even worse. From the moment I set foot in the main hallway, I was flat-out ignored. Completely and absolutely. No hellos, no nods, no nothing. No dude, no Brain, no Goldman. At least when people are making fun of you, they're paying attention. For that whole horrible week, I ate lunch alone, walked to class alone, did everything totally alone. You'll know how bad it was when I tell you that I even hoped Patrice and Archie would call. But no; I had managed to alienate not just the cool kids but the losers and freaks as well.

As you can imagine, by the time I stepped onto the plane to New York that Friday afternoon, I was desperate for something—anything—to go better. My trip definitely got off on the right foot. The flight attendants on the plane really enjoyed the fact that I was traveling alone and gave me four snack packs and two Cokes.

Then there was my dad. Angelina had made herself scarce so Dad and I could have some time alone. With a single hug at the gate, it was like everything was forgiven. First we had an early dinner. Chinese. Moo shoo pork. Orange chicken. Then we hopped on the subway to Shea Stadium. Mets vs. Cardinals, box seats, halfway up the third-base line. We won, too, on a double in the bottom of the ninth.

By the time we got back to my old apartment, I had forgotten about everything in Indiana. Who needed those jerks? My dad and I were getting along like old times, easy and loose, just like the last two months hadn't happened. After sleeping in the next morning, we went to our favorite greasy diner for eggs and bagels. Then we hurried home so I could throw on my khakis, button-down shirt, tie, and jacket for Aaron Siegel's bar mitzvah.

"Have fun, buddy," Dad said as I headed out the door. "I'll be here when you get home."

Home. I liked the sound of that.

Minutes later, I was cutting up 79th Street toward the Park Avenue Synagogue. And that is when I started to get really excited. As psyched as I had been to see my father, I was even more pumped to see my friends. Around 77th Street, I spotted some of my old gang mingling outside the synagogue, waiting to go in. Everyone was dressed up, boys in ties, girls in dresses.

Rudy Albright saw me first.

"Yo, look! It's Goldman!"

Just like that, everyone was at my side like I was some sort of rock star. I was back-patted and high-fived. And then Steve materialized out of the crowd. It was sort of weird to see him after all that time, especially after how strange things had been on the phone. But with a single hand slap, the weirdness vanished.

"Evan, buddy!"

God, did it ever feel good to have someone call me by my real name. And I'll admit that I was sort of relieved not to see Bill yet. I'd be lying if I didn't admit to having some major-league fantasies about me and Nina getting back together. Sure, I knew that she and

Bill had made out. But only because I wasn't available, right? Here's how I pictured it: With a single glance in my direction, Nina would crawl down the synagogue aisle, curl up in my lap, and whisper "I love you" in Hebrew. That's what I was thinking about while Steve and Rudy started to describe their new English teacher to me. Apparently he had a black belt in karate and could speak Russian.

"Seriously, dude," Rudy was saying. "The guy actually kicked a dictionary clean in half. He's awesome."

Pretty amazing, I supposed. But before I could respond, I heard it: A girl's voice.

Her voice.

Saying *my* name!

"Hey, Evan!"

There she was, decked out in a bright blue dress that hugged all the body parts that required hugging.

"Nina!" I gasped.

My heart went from zero to ninety in a millisecond. But then it practically exploded out of my chest. Because I saw her lips forming into a big, fat pucker. Her head was moving forward—toward me! I nearly fell over. This was happening more quickly than I had even anticipated! Thank God I had brushed my teeth after breakfast. There was nothing to do but go for it. I licked my lips and spread my arms wide.

But then . . . well, at the last second, each of us turned our head so instead of touching lips we touched cheeks. Chickened out, I guess. Aha, I thought. She doesn't want everyone to see how badly she wants me. She's saving the good stuff for later. All right, then, the day was young. All I had to do was bide my time.

"Come on," Steve said, tugging my arm. "Let's find some seats."

"See you inside," Nina said with a smile.

"Yeah," I said. "See you!"

Who ever said New York wasn't the greatest city on earth?

• • •

The Park Avenue Synagogue looked like a church in some Christmas special, except instead of stained-glass windows and pictures of Jesus there were stained-glass windows and gigantic Stars of David. It inspired awe, feeling like you were in the presence of the Lord and serious money. I was suddenly relieved that none of these people would be at my dinky little Methodist church basement ceremony a week later. Honestly, how would I explain my sorry new life if they came? How would people react?

Now that the doors were open, the place was filling fast, and I caught a glimpse of Nina taking a seat with a group of girl friends on the other side of the synagogue. I waved at her, but she didn't see it. Seconds later, Bill squeezed in next to me.

"Dude!" Bill said. "How's it hangin'?"

Despite everything I was feeling about Nina, meeting up with him and Steve was like putting on an old pair of sneakers; they just fit somehow. We began some light banter—the typical "how's school?" "how've you been?" sort of stuff. But all I wanted to do was cut to the chase: Was Bill going out with Nina? Before I could work up the nerve to ask, a cantor in a black robe led the congregation in a prayer. Then a second cantor sang a song, followed by a third who chanted a blessing. Then the rabbi himself got up. He was no geezer like Rabbi Weiner, but a young guy who looked like he should've been wearing a football helmet instead of a yarmulke.

"Today," he began, "we gather to celebrate the bar mitzvah of Aaron Guevara Siegel."

Things moved along pretty quickly after that. A few prayers later and Aaron got up to do his thing. You should've heard him: He whipped off his Torah reading like he was reciting box scores out of the sports section—the words just flowed. And his speech? It was a thing of beauty: It started with an allegory about some ancient scribe who had founded the world's first orphanage, and then it moved on to a section where he thanked his family for supporting him and loving him; it was actually very moving. Then he thanked his stepmom for being such a good friend! I debated running up to the bimah and just stealing his speech for my own ceremony next week.

In any case, as soon as the ceremony was over, Steve, Bill, and a bunch of other guys decided to walk over to the reception instead of waiting for the girls. Ten blocks later, we barged into the main lobby of the Pierre Hotel, ten obnoxious boys in suits running screaming down the elegant hallways.

I knew that Aaron's parents were rich, but this was insane. It was like their money had money. First off, the lobby had so much famous art dripping off the walls, it looked like a wing of the Met. Then we were directed down a mirrored hall, past a plush bar, and into this absolutely enormous ballroom. Waiters glided here and there with trays of appetizers and glasses of punch and champagne. A chocolate fountain pumped away into what looked like a chocolate lagoon filled with pineapple chunks and strawberries. Two huge black guys were onstage, singing and rapping, and a DJ was pounding music through the room. Tables with place cards were arranged in perfect symmetry around a glistening dance floor. On the ceiling there were four of the largest chandeliers I had ever seen. A far cry from Pam's plastic chickens.

"Let the festivities commence," Bill said. He signaled

for a waiter. "Who wants champagne?"

Steve shrugged. "I'm in."

I got nervous. "Will they let us?"

Bill shot me a glance. "This is a bar mitzvah, dude. Nobody's going to card you."

Despite everything you might hear to the contrary, most New York kids aren't drug-using sex addicts. That's only the private-school kids. When I clinked glasses with Steve and Bill and took a big swallow of champagne, I'm not embarrassed to say that it was my first drink ever. And even though we had had the typical talks in health class about the evils of alcohol, I downed the entire glass in just under a minute. Felt good, too.

"Not bad!" Bill said, putting his empty glass down and emitting an enormous belch.

"Yes sirree!" Steve said. "This hits the spot."

I grabbed a mushroom tart off a passing tray, but when I turned back, Bill was heading across the floor.

"Where you going?" Steve called.

Bill wheeled around then kept walking backward. "To find me a woman!"

I got a sick feeling in my stomach. What woman? My woman? Where was Nina, anyway? But before I had a chance to make my own move, Rudy and a gang of guys came over, and I was suddenly in the middle of a conversation about their new school.

"Wild about what happened to Mr. Henry, right?" one kid said.

"Right," Rudy said. "The dude didn't even ask permission."

"Permission for what?" I asked.

Nobody seemed to hear me.

"I know," Steve said, laughing. "And did you hear what happened in math class? You know, last Friday."

With that, the other kids broke up.

"What?" I asked.

Maybe my friends just didn't want to take the time to catch me up? Whatever the reason, I never found out what Mr. Henry did or what happened in math or about twenty other things that came up in that conversation. At first I tried to keep up, but it wasn't long before I just shut my mouth. With each word I felt farther and farther away. Had it only been a month and a half since I'd moved to Indiana? Sure, the guys had all switched schools because it was the beginning of junior high, but was it really possible for me to be so out of touch so quickly?

I slipped away when they started ragging on their new gym teacher. I had been scanning the room and finally hit pay dirt.

Nina Handleman—on the dance floor!

With a group of girl friends!

With Bill nowhere in sight!

It was all I could do not to pump my fists and shout. So what if I couldn't relate to the guys? Nina would be different. Taking her in my arms, I would tell her about the trouble with my parents, the anguish of moving, the strange people at my new school, even Archie! Yes, ours would be a love for the ages. By the time I actually reached the dance floor, it all seemed possible. Until I felt this sort of clammy hand on my shoulder.

"Hi, Evan. Remember me?"

There I was, staring down at the unfortunate face of Rachel Hadassah Zisser. Buckteeth. Black-rimmed glasses. Chin zits. Back in third grade we called her "the creature." She made up for her vastly unattractive face and figure by being unimaginably loud and irritating.

"Rachel!" I said.

That's when I noticed her embarrassingly low-cut green dress, exposing actual cleavage. Some boobs, I discovered on that day, are better left to the imagination.

"So how are. you?" Rachel said. "Tell me everything!"

I glanced at Nina. She and her friends were dancing in a circle now, taking turns shimmying into the center for solos.

"Look," I said, "I've really got to run."

"I bet you didn't know that my dad is from Lafayette," Rachel went on. "That's in Indiana too. My grandfather taught at Purdue. I love the Midwest. Everything is so clean."

As the band segued to "Hey Ya," Nina's group suddenly decided they had had enough and started wandering off the floor.

"Hey, listen, Rachel," I said. "Let's talk later, okay?"

But Rachel pivoted to block my getaway.

"Wait," she said. "I promised myself that I would do something at this party and I'm going to just do it. Just put aside my fears and go for it!"

"Oh?" I stammered.

Nina was disappearing into the crowd! I feinted to my left. Again Rachel stood her ground.

"Just give me a second, okay?" Rachel said. "Would it surprise you to hear that ever since second grade, I've had a massive crush on you? We used to play freeze tag at recess, and I just thought, That's him, that's the man of my dreams. Oh my god, I said it! I told you! Please don't hate me! I just had to tell you!"

I'm supposed to be flattered when a girl tells me she has a crush on me, right? Well, that wasn't happening.

"Listen, Rachel," I said, looking frantically over her head—disaster! Nina was nowhere to be seen!

"That's such a great thing to hear . . ."

Her eyes got wide.

"But I just . . ."

Her eyes narrowed. I could see her preparing herself for rejection.

I caught a glimpse of Nina's hair by the entrance to the ballroom.

I gulped. "You know, I'm in Indiana and everything. I just don't see how . . ."

A single tear descended Rachel's cheek. "Right. I know."

Nina was out the door.

I wanted to be kind to Rachel, but there just wasn't time. "We'll talk later, okay?" I said, and just like that I was gone, weaving and cutting through the crowd like a commuter running for a train.

"Wait!" Rachel called.

I almost knocked over a waiter with a plate of mini quiches.

"Watch it, buddy!"

Zoom, a second later I narrowly missed tackling Aaron's grandmother. But then I was at the door. I looked both ways.

At the other end of the hall! The glimmer of a blue dress! I was off like I had been shot out of a cannon. I had tasted the upper lip. Now I *needed* the lower.

Down the hall I barreled, past two wedding

receptions and another bar mitzvah party. Wait, dammit, where did she go?

I stopped.

I listened.

And then I heard her. But not her voice; her giggle. Heart racing, I turned and walked two steps to my left, and there was a staircase that headed down to a landing. And there she was. As beautiful as anyone I had ever seen. With her mouth wrapped around Bill's.

They were sucking face, lip to lip, upper and lower. And they hadn't even bothered to find someplace private.

I lurched away and meandered back down the hall. But at the door to Aaron's reception I stopped. I just couldn't go back in. Nina and Bill would inevitably return, holding hands, grinning like love-drunk fools. I felt completely out of touch with my friends. And then there would be Rachel Hadassah Zisser, circling me, waiting for another opportunity to move in for the kill.

So I walked all the way home—twenty blocks, a whole mile. I pushed open the door a half an hour or so later.

"Hey, Dad!" I called. "I'm home early!"

He had said that he would be waiting, but the apartment was strangely quiet. I flopped down on the living room sofa and turned on the television. I had never felt more alone in my life.

I heard the bedroom door creak open. Out came Dad wearing a white robe—one that Mom had gotten him for Hanukkah three years earlier.

"Hey, buddy," he said.

I didn't have to wonder why he was in a bathrobe. Angelina called from the bedroom.

"Hey, sweetie? Is it Evan?"

Dad looked at me with the same sheepish expression that had been on his face the day he told me that he and Mom were divorcing. Angelina came strutting into the room, wearing nothing but one of Dad's long dress shirts.

I stared at the TV and counted the seconds until I could get back on the plane to Indiana.

13

"BE A MAN," Rabbi Weiner had said.

I sat on the plane home from New York and tried to figure out what that meant. If there was some kind of test, I figured I was scoring in the negative numbers.

All right, I thought, to be a man must mean that I'm supposed to take responsibility for who I am and what I do. An image flashed through my mind, and once it did, it remained imprinted there like the light from a camera flash: Patrice.

• • •

Archie's mom opened the door with her phone tucked under her ear.

"Oh, you must be Evan."

I had never met the lady before, so it was strange that she knew my name. What had Archie told her about me? That I was the selfish loser from New York who moved in across the street?

"Archie will be so happy to see you," she went on. "Come on in."

I wondered if I was the only person other than Patrice to visit.

"Sure," I said. "Thanks."

Inside, Archie's mom pointed down the hall to his room. She then returned to the kitchen, leaving me to take in the living room by myself, which, I have to admit, seriously weirded me out. That's because everything in Archie's house was designed so that he could reach it. The bookcases were only five feet tall, and the walls were lined with handrails. Even stranger was the staircase. It had this little electric cart attached to a metal track—presumably so Archie could get up and down.

I'm not proud to admit it, but for a second I felt like cutting my losses and getting out of there. But like it or not, I needed Archie's help.

I heard the sounds of a fierce video game—some sort of gun battle—coming from the direction Archie's mom had pointed. So I moved cautiously down the hall. Pretty soon I was outside Archie's room. The gunfire was too loud for Archie to hear me knocking, so I just popped my head in.

I guess I hadn't ever really pictured what Archie's bedroom would look like. But once I saw it, it made perfect sense. For starters, it was absolutely trashed. The floor was littered with dirty clothes, books, CDs, DVDs, at least four different remotes, pens, crayons, comic books, candy wrappers, a box of syringes, a bottle of Pepsi, Cheetos, raisins, and what looked like a half-folded poster of Captain Picard. How he ever maneuvered through all that mess on crutches was a mystery. In the middle of the chaos was a hospital bed, this bulky, adjustable thing with railings on either side that went up and down. Next to it was an oxygen tank, standing there like a giant metal gallows.

Then there was Archie. Hunched at a desk, eyes riveted to his computer monitor, he was watching two guys battle it out with .22s. The gunfire came fast and furious.

"Hey," I said, walking tentatively into the room.

Without turning around, Archie muttered, "And so he returns."

I sighed. "Look, I need to talk to you."

To that, Archie snorted and clicked his mouse. The room was instantly filled with insanely loud music. I think Archie intended it to be threatening, but unfortunately he had clicked Anne Murray's Christmas album.

"Archie, please!" I shouted. I think the song was "Away in a Manger." "We've got to talk!"

He just sat there, staring furiously at his computer screen, banging on the arrow keys and shooting.

"Archie!"

Nothing.

I looked around and saw the plug for the computer, snaking under the desk to the outlet in the wall. I picked it up and gave it a sharp yank.

Silence.

Archie still didn't move. I perched myself on one of the few trash-free spots on his bed.

"All right," I said. "I know you're mad at me about the movie. I'm sorry I didn't have your back. I'm sorry I let you down."

Silence.

I went on: "But you weren't fair to me either, you know? Showing up at the movie like that, blaming me when I had done exactly what you asked me to do. We both were jerks. Now I'm saying I'm sorry. And I mean it."

More silence.

Should I have expected anything different?

"God, Archie! Don't you have anything to say?"

Suddenly he swiveled around in his chair.

"Okay, I agree," he said quietly. "We were both jerks. But I will continue to maintain that you were a bigger jerk than I was. If you can acknowledge that, I'll apologize."

I couldn't believe it. Me? A bigger jerk than him? It was insanity! But this was no time to get into a fight over something that idiotic.

"Fine," I said. "I was a bigger jerk than you."

Archie became so animated, I thought he was going to launch out of his seat. "Aha!" he cried. "So you agree! You *were* a bigger jerk, but I am a bigger *man*, and I can admit when I was wrong! So I'm SORRY, Evan Goldman, I'm SORRY I was a jerk, even if I was less of a jerk than you!"

With that, Archie thrust his hand forward and smiled. I half wanted to punch him. But who could stay mad at that goofy frog face? So I laughed and shook his hand. It seemed stupid not to.

"Okay, I'm sorry, too," I said.

To my surprise, it seemed like we both actually meant it. To tell the truth, I never really expected to make it that far. So I pushed forward before the whole thing blew up in my face.

"Now I need something from you," I said.

"I know already," he proclaimed. "You're moving back to New York and you want me to look in on your mom."

I shook my head. "Nope. Not moving back to New York."

Archie raised his eyebrows. "What?"

I sighed. "I don't seem to belong there anymore."

He seemed genuinely surprised. "But why not?"

"It's a long story," I said quickly. "Listen, you said you could get Patrice to be my friend again. Remember?"

Archie nodded. "True. But that was before the movie. I'm a genius, but not a miracle worker."

"Can't you try?" I asked. "It's important."

A pause. An impish grin. "I assume that this has to do with your bar mitzvah?" he said. "With becoming a man. Owning up to all the vile and rotten things you've done wrong."

Suddenly Archie sounded surprisingly like Rabbi Weiner.

I sighed. "Sort of. . . ."

Archie slapped his desk with an open palm. "I knew it! Well, if it's that important to you, I think I can make this happen!"

Shivers ran up my leg.

"You can?"

Archie rolled his chair right up to the bed and then, with great effort, hoisted himself out of the chair to sit next to me. "There has been a great disturbance in the Force."

My head was spinning. "Archie, please speak English."

"Something happened while you were gone that was not supposed to happen." Archie smiled. "Something that you need to fix."

By that point I was desperate. "Listen. I just got off a long flight from a miserable weekend and I'm not into the head games right now! Please just tell me what you're talking about!"

Archie's smile broadened into a colossal grin. "Listen closely! The love guru will speak!"

• • •

I never found out exactly how Archie knew everything he told me. But by that point I had learned not to ask. Archie had this way of lurking around and soaking up information. In any case, what follows is a semisummary of what he said that afternoon. See, while I was in New York, an event even bigger than Aaron Siegel's bar mitzvah was taking place in Appleton. The Quayle Quails were playing their archrivals, the Edgewood Thunderhawks. It was a football battle royal, featuring Brett as our knight in shining armor.

But what everyone in Appleton knew, before the game even started, was that the knight in shining armor was a little tarnished.

It all went back to *The Bloodmaster*. Turned out that little horror movie spawned a series of disasters with some far-ranging effects. Once everyone's parents found out about the R rating (not to mention all the individual lies it had taken to get out of the house), the punishments were pretty severe. Kendra's parents took away her cell phone, her computer, and her television for a whole week. Fudge and Eddie were forced to spend every day for a month going to church after football practice to clean out the sacristy. And Brett's parents took away his weight room privileges and his iPod, and signed him up for after-dinner tutoring.

Only Lucy got off scot-free. Either her parents never found out or they just didn't care. But whatever the reason, she took advantage of her relative freedom to make sure that Brett and Kendra never made up. All week long she came to cheerleading practice full of reports to Kendra about the great conversations she and Brett were having on the phone and the fabulous chats they were having online. At the same time, she made sure to remind Brett that Kendra was over him and had called him a dumb jock. Every time she said it, Brett got madder and sadder.

That's where things stood on the morning of the big game. Brett was angry at Kendra, and she was mad right back. And Lucy? She was just biding her time, ready to grab Brett for herself.

As Archie put it: "Two tongues were destined to meet. But whose?"

• • •

At the start of the game, Brett was in great form, channeling all his anger and rage into crushing the Thunderhawks. At the half the Quails were ahead 28–0. The crowd was going wild.

Throughout, Kendra was dying a slow and miserable death. But being head cheerleader wasn't just a job to her, it was a sacred duty. So she jumped, yelled, and cheered like always. She even wowed the crowd with a standing backflip. Only as the clock ticked down on the second quarter did she and Brett meet eyes. Hearts broken, they stared across the field until Kendra broke down and ran under the stands.

Then the whistle blew. Halftime.

"Okay, dude, listen," Fudge said to Brett in the locker room. "Just go talk to her. I bet she'll just give you a big ol' kiss and be so glad you're back."

Brett shook his head. "No, man, she thinks I'm just a dumb jock. She's over me."

"She's not!" Eddie said. "Have you seen her out there? Every time you turn in her direction, she bounces twice as high and screams twice as loud. She's nuts for you."

Brett blinked. "You think she still wants to be my girlfriend?"

Eddie gave Brett a playful punch on the shoulder. "Every girl in this stadium wants to be your girlfriend. Even Fudge's mother. If you want Kendra, go get her!"

With that, Brett strode out of the locker room to find his beloved.

(Again, since Archie is the one who told me this, some of the dialogue may sound a little weird. For all I know, Archie made the whole thing up. But since the end result is the same, I'm just going to pass it on and hope for the best.)

Meanwhile, Lucy was under the stands, consoling Kendra.

"I could see it his eyes," Kendra said. "He still wants me, I know he does. Why won't he talk to me?"

Lucy was all over that. "Why should he talk to you? You yelled at him about the movie, and you haven't called him all week to apologize!"

"How could I?" Kendra said. "My parents haven't let me near the phone!"

Lucy shrugged. "Sucky timing. But Brett told me yesterday that he's going to find a girl who doesn't treat him like he's stupid."

With that, Kendra started to really cry.

"It's okay," Lucy said consolingly. "Fudge is still available!"

Just then the crowd cheered. When Lucy popped her head out from the stands, she saw Brett walking right toward her—toward Kendra! Acting quickly, Lucy ran out to meet Brett on the field.

"Don't go under there!" she called.

Brett stopped abruptly. "Why? What is it?"

"Kendra," Lucy stammered. "You don't want to see it. She just ripped up a jersey with your number on it!"

Brett blinked. "She ripped up number 48?"

Lucy nodded. "And she keeps repeating that she can't understand how she ever liked such a *dumb jock*."

Brett turned red. "I'm not dumb!"

"Of course you're not, Brett! But hey, she's only trying to show off for her new boyfriend."

Brett's head virtually spun around in a full circle. His bottom lip quivered. "New boyfriend? What?"

"Him!" Lucy said and pointed to the defensive tackle on the Thunderhawks, a huge kid who was, at that moment, in the middle of doing five hundred push-ups.

"A *Thunderhawk*?"

"I'm sorry, Brett."

Brett was too full of emotion to speak. He wandered back to the locker room in a daze. Crisis averted, Lucy went back to Kendra to get her ready for the second half.

• • •

In the second half, Brett was such a mess that he could barely play the game at all. He threw three interceptions and fumbled twice. At one point he dropped back to pass, fell to the ground, and began weeping. Fudge and Eddie did all they could to pull him back together, but before anyone could get him under control, the Thunderhawks had pushed ahead. With a minute and a half left, the score was 31–28.

The Quails had one final chance. But with the ball on the fifty-yard line, Brett threw a pass ten feet over Fudge's head. Wincing in pain, he lay down on the field and yelled something.

Everyone strained to hear what he had said. Was it: Fun? Run?

What did he say?

The next play, Brett was sacked. And as he lay there, immobile, he shouted it again. This time, it was clear.

Brett had yelled "Tongue!"

"He yelled it with a heart that was cleft in two," Archie told me. "He yelled it as a symbol of every missed opportunity, every defeat, every failure the world had ever known."

"Tongue!" Brett yelled, and now the crowd understood.

One man whose wife had just left him yelled back: "Tongue!"

A woman whose daughter had just run off with a mechanic cried out: "Tongue!"

The Rasmussen twins, who had both dropped their

ice cream cones, screamed in unison: "TONGUE!"

Gradually the crowd joined in, one by one, their cry of misery and relief growing in pitch and volume, until the bleachers were full of people on their feet screaming, chanting, and barking "Tongue! Tongue! Tongue!"

Lining up for third down, the Thunderhawks watched in amazement as the crowd went collectively insane.

Then Fudge noticed something. Something about Brett. He was reveling in the crowd's response! Feeding off it! Every "tongue" seemed to restore some part of his lost soul. So Fudge began yelling it, too. And soon enough the rest of the Quails picked up the chant.

Lucy's moment had arrived. She strode onto the field, moving quickly past the ref and the Thunderhawks, right to Brett. Then before anyone could stop her, she lifted off Brett's helmet and touched his cheek. That's when Kendra screamed, but by that point the crowd had caught on and was chanting with the power of a million suns: "TONGUE! TONGUE! TONGUE!"

Lucy put her hands behind Brett's head, leaned in, and kissed him.

With tongue.

Lots of tongue.

The crowd began cheering, stomping their feet, jumping up and down with excitement.

Lucy withdrew her tongue and walked backward off the field, staring at Brett the whole time. And Brett stared back, hormones churning like mad.

Then the ref blew his whistle.

The Quails lined up at the line of scrimmage. Brett surveyed the field, looking to the Thunderhawk goal line, then narrowed his eyes.

"Hut, hut, hike!"

Snap.

Handoff.

Fake to the fullback.

Quarterback sneak!

Fifty yards for a touchdown!

The game was over. Lucy was in Brett's arms holding the game ball. Kendra was destroyed.

• • •

By the time Archie finished telling me all this (complete with impersonations of everyone involved and a surprisingly athletic attempt to show me the plays), I was standing by the window in utter shock.

"Don't you see?" He was sort of winded, to tell the truth. "Now you have to get Kendra and Brett back together!"

My eyes widened. "How can I do that?"

"Oh, it's not so hard. Look, everyone hates Lucy,

everyone loves Kendra. Brett's not stupid, he's just blinded by lust. You just have to make him see that he's picked the wrong girl."

Blinded by lust? "Archie, I can't even get to Brett. After the movie, he's pretty much sworn me off."

Archie twinkled. No, really, I swear he did. His whole being took on a weird glow like he was suddenly plugged into an outlet or something. "I know where you can find him. And it'll solve both your problems at once."

He was going too fast for me, as always.

"*Both* my problems?" I stammered.

Archie nodded. "Remember I told you that Brett's punishment for *The Bloodmaster* was getting extra tutoring?"

"Yeah?" I said.

Archie gave me a quick push.

"It's with Patrice."

And he pointed out his bedroom window toward her house. There in the yard was Brett's bike.

I collapsed on Archie's bed.

"But Brett and Patrice hate each other."

Archie shrugged. "Maybe that's part of Brett's punishment. Anyway, now you can go talk to him, and work it out with Patrice at the same time."

"But I thought *you* were going to help me work it out with Patrice."

Archie was on the floor plugging his computer back in. "I am helping you!" he said. "I already told you she's tutoring Brett!"

"How is that helpful?"

With a whir, the computer began to boot up. "Just go talk to Brett! You'll see!"

There was something else nagging at me. "Archie! If you want Kendra so badly, then why do you want her and Brett to get back together?"

"Oh, please!" Archie said. "I'm not threatened by Brett! I have my own plans!"

I was beginning to realize that, with Archie, you just had to trust whatever insane logic was going on in his head. He had a plan; he was going to see it through. Me? I had to make a quarterback see the light. And get my friendship with Patrice back.

Somehow.

I CUT through Pam's backyard and came around the back of Patrice's house. Sure enough, there was Brett. He was sitting on a screened-in porch at a patio table with an old flowered tablecloth. Patrice was across from him, waiting patiently for him to give an answer.

"Is it twelve?" he said finally.

Brett looked up from a textbook. I swear he looked as out of place doing math as I would've looked playing quarterback.

"No," Patrice said, and took a sip of tea. "Try again. But don't forget to define your variable, okay?"

Brett pushed the book away. "Easy for you to

say. I just can't do this."

"You're just not concentrating," Patrice said.

Of course he couldn't concentrate, I thought. He's trying to figure out whether he should be going out with the hottest girl in school or the second-hottest girl in school.

"Yo, what's he doing here?"

Busted! I guess I had been so stunned by the sight of Patrice and Brett together that I had just stood there gaping. Not that I had any great plan of what to say or do once I arrived, but it still would've been nice to have had a decent opening line.

"Hey, Brett. Hey, Patrice."

Brett sighed heavily. Patrice scowled, but I could've sworn she blushed a little bit first. Anyway, with no one to stop me, I let myself through the screen door.

"So, Brain?" Brett said with a smile. "Did you come back from New York so you could tell me I'm an idiot too?"

Patrice pointed at the problem he was working on. "You're not an idiot, Brett, you're just not paying attention."

"Well, I have a lot on my mind," he said, and grabbed his football jacket. "Come to think of it, now that Brain's here, maybe I should beat it." He smiled. "I have better things to do than hang out at a freak convention."

My heart took a giant lurch nearly clear out of my chest. I had to act fast.

"Wait!" I said.

Brett faced me. "Yeah?"

I swallowed hard. A million thoughts were going through my head, but I couldn't think of a single thing to say. So I blurted out the first thing I could think of.

"Hey, I heard about you and Lucy. Congratulations."

Brett took a step toward me. "What's that supposed to mean?"

"Nothing," I stammered. Was "congratulations" a bad word in Indiana? "Just that I hear you two are going out. That's great, right?"

I saw Patrice out of the corner of my eye. She looked sort of amused, like she was enjoying watching me fight for my life. In any case, Brett paused a minute, as if he were considering whether dating Lucy was really all that great or not.

"Yeah, it's great," he said finally.

With that, he grabbed his textbook and pushed through the screen door.

"Brett, wait!" I called. It was time for some more quick thinking. "I need your advice!"

One foot in Patrice's backyard, he turned. "You need advice from me?" He smirked. "Last I heard, *you* were the Brain."

"Maybe," I said. I met his eyes. "But this is advice about a girl. And you know more about that than anyone."

Finally Brett looked interested. After some wild improvising, I had stumbled onto the right tack.

"A girl, huh?" he asked. "Someone in New York?"

I glanced quickly at Patrice, who was pretending to be deeply engrossed in her algebra book.

"It doesn't matter who it is," I said, looking back at Brett. "I made a mistake and I need to fix it."

Something very sad crossed Brett's eyes. That's when I knew I really had him hooked—for the next minute or two anyway.

"What'd you do?" he asked.

I sat down at the table. Patrice kept her nose in the book, but I could tell she was listening.

"I made the wrong choice about something." I paused. "I mean, I did something really stupid to this girl, and I'm afraid I've lost her."

Leaning against the door frame, Brett drew in a deep breath. "Yeah, I know about that kind of thing."

I shrugged. "So I've been trying to figure out what to do."

I guess this was all getting to be a bit much for Patrice. Suddenly she was on her feet. "Tutoring's over," she said. "I better get going."

Brett smiled. "You can't—it's your house."

Patrice's face dropped.

"Besides," Brett said, "I have an idea! Maybe you can help the Brain with his problem!" He winked at me. "Come on, Patrice. Sit!"

What other choice did she have? Brett took his seat again, too.

"Look, Brain," he said. "What would you say if *I* was the one who made the stupid mistake and lost my girl, and I was coming to *you* for advice?"

I thought Patrice snorted.

I sighed, maybe a little theatrically. This was actually the perfect opening. "Well, I'd say . . . if she's really important to you, then you should just . . . tell her."

"Tell her?" Brett said. He thought that over for a moment. "Tell her what?"

Suddenly Patrice was looking straight at me. "Yeah, Evan. What should he say?"

It was the first time she had spoken to me since the movie. I had forgotten how soft she could look when she wasn't angry. I felt my face flush.

"Come on, Brain," Brett said. "Time's a-wasting."

I felt just like I had before I jumped into the quarry. No doubt about it: I was being challenged. So I gulped and dove in.

"Tell her that you haven't stopped thinking about her since it happened. And that you know you were wrong."

Brett nodded. "Yeah, that's good."

"Tell her that you made a decision under a lot of pressure," I said. "Then say if you had it to do all over again, you would never have made that choice."

"Never," Brett echoed.

I didn't dare look at Patrice—not directly. But out of my peripheral vision, I could see her looking right at me. So I swallowed and kept going. "Tell her . . . tell her that you got scared. And people do dumb things sometimes when they're scared, but that's not an excuse. There is no excuse. There's only hoping that she'll forgive you. Because you're so sorry that you hurt her."

I held my breath, ready to make a dash into the woods if things got too strange.

"This is good stuff," Brett said with a nod. He was actually scribbling notes on the inside cover of his textbook. Then to my surprise, Patrice jumped in.

"That's not everything," she said.

Brett raised his eyebrows. "Oh?"

Patrice nodded again. "Tell her that even though she did some things that made you really mad, you always knew how much she cared about you."

"It's true," Brett said with a nod. He jotted another note. "That's very true."

But Patrice wasn't finished. "And tell her that the time you spent together was so great, and so much fun, that it hurt even more when she stopped talking to you."

I looked right at her but spoke to Brett. "Also let her know that you know it can't ever be the same. But maybe it can be even better if you two forgive each other."

I could tell that Patrice was working up the nerve to look at me, but she just couldn't. So she addressed her next thought to the woods behind her house. "Tell her that you haven't been able to watch an old movie for weeks."

Brett looked up, confused. "But Kendra and I don't watch old movies."

"Just go with it, Brett!" Patrice said, hitting him on the shoulder.

Genuinely surprised, Brett said, "All right, I'm going with it! Old movies!"

I reached my hand across the table toward her. "Tell her you'd do anything for a second chance."

Patrice looked down at my hand. Finally she looked up. Her eyes were full of tears. Then she placed her hand in mine.

That's when I heard a sniffle. Patrice and I both turned to see Brett wiping away tears of his own. When he noticed us looking, he jumped up from the table.

"Good stuff, Brain! See? You don't need my advice

at all! You can do it all yourself! Just tell her!" He bolted for the door. "I've gotta go find someone!"

Moments later, we heard the sound of his bike zooming down the driveway.

Patrice and I were alone. I looked down, surprised to see that our hands were still touching. I didn't move mine. She didn't move hers. Then Patrice smiled.

"You're such a jerk," she said.

I smiled right on back. "You're a pain in the ass."

She laughed. "I know."

We looked at each other for a long time. Every once in a while one of us would laugh, or start crying, but we didn't stop looking.

Finally she pulled her hand away.

"So," she said. "Now can I come to your stupid bar mitzvah?"

According to the Talmud, today is the day I become a man. And what I've learned is that being a man isn't just growing older, it's growing up. It's taking responsibility, it's acknowledging who you are and what you want, and if you do it right, you end up finding out where you belong. Becoming a man is

THE PHONE rang in the kitchen. Pam got up from the couch and waddled in and picked it up. I tried to keep working on my speech, but an actual ringing phone was such a rare occurrence in that house that I couldn't help but be curious. Had to be my dad calling to find out what I'd told Mom about the weekend in New York.

Except it wasn't.

Pam called for my mom, and when she picked up, I could tell from the tone of her voice that she couldn't be talking to Dad at all. Pam came back and sat next to me.

"Well, that's very thoughtful of you to ask," Mom said. Her voice had that sugary sweet tone I had heard once when we ran into my old principal on Lexington Avenue. "You know, while it's a big party for everyone, it's also a religious ceremony, so I think the kids should dress modestly and respectfully."

I was on my feet in a second flat. Who could she be talking to? It had to be about my bar mitzvah, but outside of Patrice, there were no kids coming!

"No, no, I'll make sure there are yarmulkes for the boys—you won't have to worry about that. Very sweet of you to ask." A pause. "Bring? Oh, you don't have to bring anything. We'll just be thrilled that you and Malcolm are there."

Malcolm?

As in Fudge?

The kid who had goaded me into jumping into a quarry, pushed me at gym, then given me a wedgie for the record books? No, Mom couldn't be talking to Fudge's mother—that made no sense. Was there some other Malcolm I'd invited?

"Yes, of course, Mrs. Venter, looking very much forward to it!"

Venter was Fudge's last name! This had to be a prank. All the kids would pretend they were coming, then not show at the last minute.

Mom hung up. "Well!" she yelled out from the kitchen. "Isn't that lovely?"

My mouth was having trouble forming the word "What?" so I just looked at her hoping her next sentence would explain everything.

She didn't get a chance, because the doorbell rang. Simon barked and jumped up. Mom and I exchanged a glance like "Who's ringing the doorbell at nine o'clock on a Sunday night?" and Pam groaned and got off the couch to open the door.

I did not expect to hear "Whoa, those voodoo masks are wiggin' me out!"

I did not expect to hear "Hey, Miss Pam, is Evan around?"

I certainly did not expect that the people saying those things would be Brett and Kendra, who then walked into the house with their arms wrapped around each other's waists.

"The Brain!" shouted Brett as he saw me. I stood up and waved, utterly mystified as Simon slapped Brett's belly with his paws.

"All right, easy, buddy," he said.

"Oh my god, Miss Pam," Kendra said, staring in wonder at the naked statues, "this house is soooooo cool!"

I quickly gathered my composure. "Mom, this is Brett and Kendra."

Mom shook their hands. "It's so nice of you both to drop by tonight."

Pam raised an eyebrow. "Isn't it a little late on a school night for you to be out?"

Brett laughed. "It's cool—we just wanted to thank the Brain for helping us out."

"What did I do?" I said, feeling more nervous than proud.

My mom grabbed Pam. "Let's go get some coffee in the kitchen," she said, and pulled Pam out of the room. Simon collapsed on the rug.

"What did you do?" Kendra asked. She sat down on the couch, and Brett flopped down happily next to her. "Evan, you completely saved the day!"

"I did?"

"Dude," Brett said, "you told me this afternoon that I had to own up to making a mistake and just ask for a second chance, and I did. I just went over to Kendra's house and I was like, 'I'm sorry, please forgive me.'"

"And I didn't want to forgive him," Kendra interrupted, "but look at that face!" With that, she cupped his face in her hands and kissed him. I was glad they were happy, but I didn't really need to be watching it.

"I told her I would never have had the guts to talk to her if it weren't for you . . ."

". . . And so I said we had to come over and thank you!"

Brett lifted his hand in the air. I high-fived him.

Kendra elbowed Brett. "And . . ."

Brett looked puzzled. "What?" Another elbow from Kendra. A look of recognition passed over Brett's face. "Oh, right! Dude! So we're all gonna come on Saturday!"

My eyebrows shot over my forehead. A smile immediately began in the center of my face and stretched out to the ends of my ears. I was so happy, it felt like my hair was dancing. "You're *all* coming?"

Kendra laughed. "All of us! Eddie, Fudge, everyone at school."

"I already called them all and told them we're going," Brett said.

So that explained the phone call from Fudge's mom.

"Wow, you guys," I said, "this is great. I mean, I really didn't do anything."

Brett nodded thoughtfully. "Nah, you did, Brain. You owned up to who you were. I saw you with Patrice. That was heavy."

Kendra's eyes went wide. "Wait! That's so cute! Patrice needs a boyfriend *so bad*."

"Well, we're not going out," I protested.

"It won't be lllllllllllllong!" Brett yelled, sticking out his tongue and wagging it triumphantly.

I shook my head, but I'd be lying if I said the thought hadn't occurred to me. I mean, I was practically thirteen. Maybe it was time to graduate to two lips. Anyway, just then Kendra glanced at the time on her phone.

"Brett, we gotta cruise," she said. "See you tomorrow, Evan!"

I hadn't stopped smiling. To tell the truth, I thought I never would. "Yeah," I said, "I'll see you all at school tomorrow!"

Brett opened the door, and he and Kendra walked out of the house and got on their bikes. Then I remembered one last thing I needed to do.

"Kendra, wait!"

I ran outside into the front yard. Simon waited at the front door.

"What's up, Brain?" Brett shouted across the lawn.

"I have to ask Kendra a quick favor," I said. "Sort of in private?"

They looked at each other and shrugged, and Kendra got off her bike and walked up the lawn to meet me.

"What's up?" she said.

I looked at the house across the street. I could see the light was still on in Archie's room. I hoped he wasn't watching.

"Okay, listen," I said quietly. "You remember Archie?"

"Archie? You mean the creepy crippled kid at the movie?"

I took a deep breath. "Look, Archie's not really creepy, he's just lonely. And maybe he's a little angry at the world because he's sick."

Kendra wrinkled her brow. "What's he have, anyway?"

"Some muscular thing," I said. I paused and took another quick glance up at his window. "I don't remember exactly what it's called, but I don't think he's gonna get better. And the one thing he wants more than anything in the world is . . ."

Now that I was so close, I had trouble spitting out the words.

"What?" Kendra said.

"To go on a date with you."

Kendra's eyes went wide. Then she turned to Brett, as if to make sure he hadn't overheard. Only when she saw that he was busy playing a game on his phone did she look back at me.

"What do you mean, a date?"

She looked pretty skeptical. It was hard to blame her.

"I mean like you two could meet at Dairy Queen and he'd buy you an ice cream cone and he'd sit there and tell you about *The Lord of the Rings* or something, and all you'd have to do is nod and say yes, and it would make him the happiest kid in the whole world."

"This sounds weird," Kendra said.

I laughed. "It *is* weird, but it's true. He just wants to know that for one day in his life, you paid attention to him."

"Evan . . ."

"Would you do that for me? Please? It's half an hour, and then it's all over."

She looked at her nails. She looked at the stars, then back at Brett. "You did a really great thing for us, Evan. . . . Okay, I'll go on a 'date' with Arnold."

"Archie," I corrected her.

"Ha, okay; Archie. I'll do it."

"Thank you, Kendra! You're the best!"

"But don't tell anyone about it, okay?" she said as she walked back to her bike.

I walked with her. "I'll talk to you later this week and we'll figure out the details."

Brett closed his phone. "All set?"

"All set," Kendra said, smiling.

"See you tomorrow!" Brett yelled as they drove off.

I would like to tell you that I was dignified and calm, but at that moment I jumped up in the air and punched the sky and danced all around the front lawn in the glare of the one streetlight on our block. I wrestled Simon, kicked my feet up in the air, and sang a silent celebratory march.

I had done it! All the cool kids were coming to my bar mitzvah, AND I had fulfilled my promise to Archie, AND Patrice and I were friends again. I envisioned what my bar mitzvah was going to look like:

Kendra dancing.

Patrice hanging out with everyone and enjoying it.

Brett and the Goons lifting me up in a chair.

Bill and Steve calling from New York and not being able to get through because I'm having too much fun to pick up the phone.

Mom and Dad sitting together, laughing as they watch everyone having such a great time. Maybe he tentatively puts his hand on hers. Maybe she takes it. Maybe they kiss.

Angelina deciding that Pam is more her type and leaving my dad.

Rabbi Weiner shaking his booty to some Eminem.

Indiana may not be the best place in the world, but at that moment I knew I could survive it; no, I could transcend it. In Indiana maybe I could be a man after all.

I wanted to run over to Archie and tell him what was going on, but just as I turned toward his house, I saw the light in his room go off.

Oh well, I thought. I'll tell him tomorrow.

"Come on, Simon," I yelled.

I picked up a stick and threw it as far as I could. He went tearing after it, and we played fetch all the way over to Main Street and back.

AND THEN I got punched in the face.

Not right away, of course. It took a whole day to happen, but looking back, by the time I went to bed Sunday night, my face was already on a collision course with a very large fist.

I suppose if Mom hadn't let me sleep in on Monday morning, I might have dodged it. I guess she thought something like "He's had a rough weekend with the trip back to New York and he's got a big week coming up with his bar mitzvah on Saturday, so what could be the harm in letting him sleep a little later?" So I didn't get to school until the middle of lunch, and by the time I gave my note to the guidance counselor, it was too late to go out to the parking lot to meet the gang, so I wandered over to the cafeteria. It was great, for once, knowing that I could talk to anybody I wanted. After all, I had saved the day! Brought Brett and Kendra together! Nobody could say I wasn't cool now.

Standing in the cafeteria, holding my tray of pasta, oatmeal cookies, and milk, I looked around for Patrice and Archie. But it was later than I had thought. They had already left. I glanced at the clock—only five minutes left to find a place to sit and wolf my food. That's when I realized that something weird was going on. At first I thought I was just being paranoid. But then I'd walk past a table and everyone would suddenly become intensely interested in their spaghetti. And when I finally sat down, all the kids at the table got very quiet, then got up one by one and wandered away.

It got even weirder. After lunch three kids flattened themselves against the lockers when I walked past them. When I rounded the corner by the music lab, a group of girls stopped talking altogether and ran, giggling like crazy, into the girls' room. In chorus I whispered "What's going on?" to this fat kid with a squeaky high voice named Alex Crayton, but he just raised his eyebrows and slid farther down the bench.

It was like I had been transported into one of those

old *Twilight Zone* episodes where everything was upside down. And where were Archie and Patrice?

• • •

I was really relieved when Kendra and Lucy ran over to me before math. Kendra smiled like only she could. "Hey, Ev!"

"Kendra! Lucy!"

Both girls seemed downright overjoyed to be in my presence. Of course, I could understand it about Kendra. After all, I had gotten her back together with Brett. But Lucy was a different story.

"This is so cool," she said, stopping by my side. "I'm glad we're all friends again."

It seemed she was taking the news about Kendra and Brett surprisingly well. Maybe Lucy was a better person than I had given her credit for? Maybe Kendra's friendship meant more to her than dating Brett?

"Yeah," I said. "Me, too."

Kendra nodded. "For what it's worth, Brett's glad we're friends, too."

Lucy smiled. "You know, he really looks up to you, Evan."

It was cool to hear that the school hero looked up to me.

"I don't know about that," I said, shrugging. "I'm just glad everything worked out."

"Oh, wait!" Kendra shouted. Suddenly she was tugging on my shirtsleeve. "We have to do that thing!"

Lucy's ears perked up. "What thing?"

"No, me and Evan! Look," she said to me, "I owe you that favor. What do I have to do?"

I knew she was talking about the date she'd agreed to go on with Archie. Meanwhile, I noticed that everyone in the hall was edging away from us. I was so distracted that I didn't really concentrate on what Lucy said next.

"Hey, if you two want to talk about something privately, why don't you meet after school?"

I didn't think we needed a private meeting to arrange a time for Kendra and Archie to hook up. But Kendra seemed to think it was a good idea. And Lucy pushed it.

"Lunchroom after school?" she said to me and Kendra. "Brett'll be at practice."

If I had been paying attention, I might have heard the warning signs. But I was so happy to be back in the winner's circle that I didn't really notice anything else.

"Okay," I said. "The lunchroom after school. Cool."

Kendra agreed. Moments later, she and Lucy trotted off, leaving me alone. I looked around. Owen

Partington, this kid I knew vaguely from English, was the only other person left in the hallway. He was staring at me, pale as a sheet.

"What's up with you?"

His lower lip was shaking. "You're a brave man, Evan Goldman. A brave man and a fool."

And he grabbed his backpack and ran off down the hall as fast as he could.

• • •

My cell phone was on vibrate during math. As Ms. Fitzgerald droned on about quadratic equations, I felt it buzz to tell me there was a text waiting. Then, no more than thirty seconds later, it buzzed again. Remembering the rules about cell phones in school, I tried to ignore it. But five minutes later it buzzed again. When another text came in three minutes later, I pulled the phone out of my back pocket to see who it was. Before I could even read the display, Ms. Fitzgerald's hand was in my face.

"You know the rules, Mr. Goldman."

Reluctantly I handed it over, expecting to hear everyone in class laughing. Instead, dead silence. Sensing something behind me, I whirled around in my seat. There were Fudge and Eddie, staring me down. Then Eddie drew his finger across his throat. I gasped. What had gotten into everyone? Was he saying I was a dead man? Hadn't they all said they were coming to my bar mitzvah?

The minute the bell rang, I turned to ask Eddie and Fudge what was going on, but they bolted like a couple of racehorses out of the starting gate, and I got cut off by the swarm of kids pushing for the door. Why was everyone acting like I had leprosy all of a sudden? This place was so weird.

"Uh, Mr. Goldman?"

I turned. There was Ms. Fitzgerald holding out my phone. But it wasn't so easy to get it back. I had to promise up, down, and sideways that I'd never bring it into class again. Which was seriously irritating. For starters, I was dying to see who was sending me those texts. It was also time to meet Kendra. Anyway, by the time I finally got it back, I was practically shaking. I scrolled to the message icon and pressed Texts and then inbox. Patrice!

I knew I had to get to the lunchroom fast, so while I ran down the stairs, I clicked on the last text and started to scroll back through her messages in reverse order.

I'm serious Evan don't do it!

Don't do what? I bolted out of the stairwell and raced down the hallway. The text before that read:

Please! Call me! Why aren't you calling me?

Rounding the corner to the cafeteria, I tripped and sprawled flat on my face. My phone flew out my hands and skittered across the linoleum tiles, shedding pieces of plastic until it crashed into the concrete wall. Disaster! Even if I could have turned it on, the screen was cracked beyond the point of visibility.

Why was my day going so wrong? I was supposed to be the hero of the school!

The only person in the lunchroom was Kendra, sitting and listening to her iPod, drumming her fingers on the table. I slipped my ruined phone into my pocket and hurried in.

"Hey, Ken!"

She took the earphones out and smiled. A smile like that, I'll tell you, makes up for a lot of bad days.

"Hey, Evan."

I sat across from her. "Do you know why is everyone acting so weird?"

Kendra looked confused. "What do you mean? I haven't noticed anything."

How could she not have noticed? But then I remembered. Kendra could be sitting in the middle of a hurricane and not feel the breeze.

"So," Kendra said. She took out her BlackBerry. "When should we do this meeting with Arnold?"

"Archie," I corrected her gently. "I think it should

be before my bar mitzvah. Like, maybe, Friday after school?"

She looked at her BlackBerry and twirled her hair. "I've got cheerleading practice . . . and then Brett and I are supposed to hang out. . . . I don't know."

In the distance, I heard a bunch of kids yelling. I decided to ignore it. "Okay, what about Thursday?"

"Hmmmmm." Apparently Thursday wasn't going to work either. "I've got cheerleading practice, and then I'm supposed to hang out with Brett . . . but maybe . . ."

The kids yelling were getting closer. And they were chanting something. At first I thought it was "Strike! Strike!"

"Okay, Wednesday after school I've got cheerleading practice, but after that . . . oh, no, wait, Brett and I were going to hang out."

It wasn't "Strike!"

It was "Fight! Fight! Fight!"

The door burst open, and I heard the sound of what seemed like over two hundred kids yelling their heads off. And what I saw was Brett, in his football uniform, coming right at me.

"Get away from her!"

Kendra looked up cheerfully.

"Hey, Brett!"

Before I even could make sense of what was going

on, Brett's right hand was around my throat and I felt myself being lifted into the air.

"What are you doing with him?" Brett shouted at Kendra.

Her expression changed abruptly.

"Brett, put him down!"

"I said what are you doing with him?"

By that point I could barely breathe. I started flailing, and Brett threw me to the ground.

"Brett," I gasped. "We were just talking—"

"You expect me to believe that?"

"I'm not gonna fight you, Brett." I slid backward away from him. "I don't know what's going on!"

Brett kicked a chair out of the way.

"Get up, Brain. No more games."

"Brett! We were just talking."

He pulled me up by my shirt. "I said GET UP!"

The crowd cheered, then even louder when Brett slammed me into a cart, sending napkins and straws flying.

"You steal my girl, Brain? Some friend! Let's go, let's do it!"

"Brett, please!"

Now I understood why everyone had been avoiding me. Somehow the word had got around that even though I had gotten Brett and Kendra back together, I had been secretly hooking up with Kendra, and every-

one knew that Brett would kill me if he heard about
it. Which he obviously had. But how?

I looked at everyone staring at me.

Then I noticed who was missing.

Lucy.

Of course. She'd started the rumor that morning.
This was her revenge.

"Please, Brett, stop!" Kendra shouted, standing on
top of the table.

"Oh, yeah? Is that how it is?" Brett's nostrils were
flaring, and his eyes were blazing. "You want me to
take it easy on your boyfriend?"

"Oh my god, we were just talking! Brett!"

That's when I got punched. Hard, too. I crumpled
to the floor, and Kendra screamed. And Brett? I guess
he felt bad. Or realized that he might get in trouble,
because he pushed through the crowd and ran. And
everyone followed. Not a single person came over to
see if I was okay. Before long, the only person left with
me was Kendra, who was hugging herself, stunned
and in tears. My nose was bleeding, and I could feel
the whole right side of my face swelling up like a bal-
loon. I curled up into a ball and closed my eyes.

DINK clump.

DINK clump.

DINK clump.

DINK clump.

"I heard someone say you guys were here!"

I would've thought that even Archie would notice that the room had been torn apart and that I was in a fetal position on the floor.

"It's perfect!" he went on.

I looked up. To my surprise, he was taking his computer out of his book bag and putting it on a table.

"Kendra, I wrote something for you!"

She hadn't even registered his presence. In fact, she hadn't registered much of anything. But as Archie pulled a bulky pair of headphones out of his bag and plugged them into his laptop, she slowly began to emerge from her stupor.

"You're gonna love it!" he crowed.

I barely managed to croak, "Archie, what are you doing?" but I knew before I said it that he wasn't listening.

Kendra looked down and took in the scene. She looked completely mystified to see Archie standing before her. At that moment he held the headphones out to her.

"Listen! Listen to it! You'll really like it!"

Kendra slowly put her BlackBerry in her book bag, slung her bag over her shoulder, and stood there uncertainly. Then she looked at me. I caught her eye. I wished I could explain to her about Lucy, about what had happened, but I knew she wouldn't get it. It would never have occurred to her that her best friend could have set her up like that. Looking into her face, I realized that I had never seen anyone look that sad in my entire life.

"Kendra?" Archie was balancing on his crutches and holding out the headphones.

She never even looked at him—just turned and walked out of the lunchroom.

"Kendra!"

He yelled it after her, at first still sounding happy, excited; then another time, but more upset. Then scared.

"Kendra!"

And then devastated.

"Kendra!"

She wasn't coming back.

Archie looked at me for the first time. I couldn't believe what he said next.

"What did you do to her?"

I rolled onto my back. "Oh, Archie, please, I didn't do anything."

Didn't he notice the blood dripping down my chin and onto my shirt?

"She's gone," he said. "I wrote her a song and she's gone."

I propped myself up on my elbows. "You wrote her a song?"

He stared off in the direction Kendra had gone.

"Do you even sing?" I asked, but as I said it, I knew it was a mistake.

Archie turned on me. "You were supposed to help me out! You know I couldn't meet her any other way. And now you're letting her walk away!"

I slumped back to the floor and closed my eyes.

"I did help you," I muttered. "That's what Kendra and I were talking about before all this . . ."

I don't even know if he heard me. By that point, he was looking down the hallway to where she had left.

"She was supposed to listen to my song! What am I going to do now?"

You could help me get up, I thought, but that seemed unlikely. Then he started clomping after her.

"Archie, come back," I said weakly.

I watched him walk out the door. When I noticed that he had left his computer and book bag behind, I almost called after him. But then I got curious. I crawled across the floor, pulled the headphones down, and put them on. Then I felt around for the keyboard. I touched the space bar, and the headphones filled with the sound of an orchestra.

I recognized it immediately; it was a section from Anne Murray's Christmas record! But Archie had played with it somehow, stretched it out and repeated it and added in a drumbeat, turning it from "Good King Wenceslas" into something entirely new.

And then there was Archie's voice. Singing. Well, I wouldn't call it singing, exactly, but it had notes and rhythms. And more importantly, it had words. I had never heard Archie sound so gentle or so . . . sincere.

This is what he sang:

I think you saw me at the back of the lunch line.
Someone tripped me when you walked by.
I think you saw me Tuesday morning in English,
'Cause you smiled when I mumbled "Hi."
I guess you saw me at the movie last weekend,
And it all turned out wrong.

But I know you won't change who you are;
I want you to stay the same.
I don't expect miracles,
I just want you to know my name.

I spend a lot of time just hoping for something
In a world full of don'ts and can'ts.
But any time I feel afraid or defeated,
I just think of the way you dance.
And I imagine that I'm dancing beside you
To a beautiful song.

And I know you won't change who you are;
I want you to stay the same.

I don't expect miracles,
I just want you to know my name.

My name is Archie.
I think you're beautiful.
And I would die if you looked at me
The way that I look at you.

You're what a miracle looks like
So I thought you should know my name.

The music stopped. I leaned back against the table with my eyes closed. I couldn't quite believe it: Archie had created something beautiful and honest. He had told Kendra how he felt and exposed everything in his soul, and he had done it in the only way he knew how.

And I knew, sitting there on the lunchroom floor, that she would probably never hear it.

"There you are! Oh, my god!"

I opened my eyes. My mother was rushing toward me.

"Are you all right? What did that monster do to you?"

"I'm okay," I said, though I doubt I was very convincing.

Next thing I knew, I felt Mom put her arms around me and help me up. I collapsed into her arms then onto the lunchroom bench.

Then I felt someone else gently take my hand. I looked up and saw Patrice sitting next to me. There we were, me, Mom, and Patrice. I managed a weak smile, and Mom and Patrice helped me to my feet and led me out of the school.

"THAT'S IT, I'm canceling the whole thing!"

My mother was ranting in the car on the way back from the emergency room. I was fine, by the way, nothing broken, just a lot of bruises and a major black eye.

"I don't know what I was thinking, coming out here! Of course you got beat up! You're smart, you're handsome, and they're just a bunch of animals!"

Patrice was immensely relieved when we dropped her off at her house. By then Mom was completely losing it.

"Anti-Semites! You come out here to the middle of the country, and you're surrounded by Jew-haters!"

I think she wanted to avoid offending Pam, so she cooled off a little by the time we got to the house. We ate dinner pretty much in silence, but as Pam got out a carton of ice cream for dessert, Mom couldn't hold back anymore.

"You know," she said, "it's the football thing. They're all taught to be violent! To be aggressive!"

Pam and I exchanged a glance.

"Ruth," Pam said gently, "we're all sorry about what happened, but Evan's perfectly safe here."

Mom shook her head. "With these mouth-breathing knuckle-dragging apes?"

"Mom," I said. "Easy."

But she was on a roll. "And I was going to let you have your bar mitzvah here? They'll bomb the ceremony! They're terrorists! Illiterate anti-Semitic terrorists!"

It was time to stop the insanity. "Come on, Mom," I said. "This wasn't about being Jewish. Brett would have done this no matter what religion I was. He just got caught up in a stupid rumor and he hit me. That's all."

"That's all?" Mom shrieked. "We're canceling the whole thing. You can go back to New York and have the bar mitzvah with your father while I figure out where we can go to be safe."

I almost choked on my spoon. A few weeks back I

would've killed to hear something like that. But things had changed. I felt suddenly exhausted.

"No," I said.

Mom blinked. "No?"

"Listen," I said, "I don't want to spend any more time feeling like everything's up in the air. I didn't want to leave New York to be in this crazy place, but we did. And now that we did, I want to see it through. No one's going to beat me up. To tell the truth, no one even cares that I'm alive anymore. So let's just have the bar mitzvah. You, me, Pam, Patrice, and Rabbi Weiner. If no one else comes, that's fine. I need to do this already, okay? Get it over with and move on. We all need to move on."

Pam nodded. "He's right, Ruth. It'll be fine."

A tear rolled down Mom's cheek. I felt bad about everything she had been through, but I still couldn't help smiling at how strange life could be. Had I really just talked my mother into letting me get bar mitzvahed in Appleton, Indiana?

• • •

I suppose I should catch you up on the rest of the week. For starters, I didn't go to school on Tuesday or Wednesday. Mom was busy having conferences with the principal and the guidance counselors, and I was busy convalescing. I didn't feel that bad physically, but I looked like hell. By the end of the day Wednesday,

Mom figured out that nobody was going to punish Brett, the Football Hero, and she asked me if I really felt comfortable going back to school.

"If anyone tries to take a swing at me, I'll just recite my haftorah at them."

She laughed a little and closed the door.

I went back to Dan Quayle Thursday morning, and it was just as I expected: completely uneventful. Nobody threatened me, nobody mocked me. In fact, nobody talked to me or really even acknowledged that I was alive. I was wallpaper. Sure, a few teachers asked how I was and acted concerned, but that was it. To be honest, I was grateful not to get the attention. After school, Patrice waited for me and we walked home together so I didn't have to take the bus.

She told me what I had already assumed: Kendra never really figured out what Lucy had done and they were still best friends. Meanwhile, Brett and the Goons had begun paying attention to two other girls on the cheerleading squad, and everyone figured Brett would be going out with Kelly Migliaccio soon. Word was that Kelly had done more than just the tongue with a kid in high school.

Patrice also said she was standing by her locker once near Kendra when Brett walked by. Apparently the two of them glared at each other the entire time they were in proximity, but neither one said a word.

As for Archie, nobody had seen him all week. I saw the lights go on and off in his bedroom across the street, but he wasn't looking out his window or waiting for the bus. For all intents and purposes, he had vanished. So Thursday afternoon, Patrice and I both stopped at his house and rang the bell. His mother answered.

"Hi, kids," she said, the phone resting on her shoulder. "This really isn't a good time."

"We just wanted to say hi to Archie," I said. "Is he here?"

Archie's mom put the phone to her ear. "One second, Dr. Mars," she said, and then she turned back to us. "I'll tell him you came by, okay?"

"Okay," Patrice said, "but . . ."

"This is really not a good time, sweetie," she repeated, and closed the door as she went back to her call. Patrice and I stood on the front step, not sure what to think or feel.

That night I had one last lesson with Rabbi Weiner. He asked me if I had my speech ready. "I will by Saturday," I said, though I didn't really believe it.

• • •

The morning of the big day I woke early and wandered over to the mirror. The swelling was down a bit, but I still had a black eye that hurt a little when I touched it.

As I was heading to the bathroom to brush my teeth, I saw a suit hanging on the back of my door. It was gray with pinstripes, just like Aaron Siegel's. I have to admit it, I was pretty touched. Pam must've stayed up half the night altering it. I figured it cost my mom a fortune.

So I put on the suit, and I tied the red tie Pam had ordered for me. Then I put on one of the two hundred personalized yarmulkes Mom had ordered back when she assumed there was going to be a crowd. Then we all went down to the Methodist church.

In the short car ride over it really hit me.

My bar mitzvah.

Finally.

I had spent so long thinking about it, strategizing about it, and worrying about it, that it was hard to believe it was finally here. Sure, the church basement would be emptier than a pool party at Rachel Zisser's, but given that I looked like I'd been run over by a bus, that was just fine by me. Four people, or forty, I'd still become a man.

• • •

I recognized Rabbi Weiner's old Volkswagen in the parking lot, and I saw Patrice's dad's Volvo, but some of the other spots in the lot were filled with cars that I had never seen. And in the handicapped spot right near the door there was a Ford Focus with Florida license plates that seemed weirdly familiar.

We got out of the car, and Mom turned to look at me.

"Okay, kiddo," she said. She straightened my tie and pushed my hair out of my eyes. "You're gonna be great. I'm so proud of you."

I noticed she was trying not to cry, so I got completely embarrassed and shook her off. Let's not get sentimental about it, I thought. I'm gonna speak some Hebrew, I'm gonna kiss a Torah, we're gonna drink a cup of red wine, and then we're all done. I pushed open the door to the church and headed down the stairs to the basement.

But just as I was about to push open the basement door, I stopped. Coming from inside were voices—a lot of them, too—talking and laughing. Instantly I thought of the strange cars in the lot. Great—someone else booked the room this morning and didn't tell us.

But then I heard a sound that made no sense in Appleton. A man telling a joke in Yiddish. Not just a man. My grandfather!

I pushed open the door and stopped short, staggered by what I saw. The basement was full of my family.

"There he is!"

That was Dad's dad, Grandpa Joel.

"The bar mitzvah boy!"

Grandma Anna.

Mom's parents were there too, along with my father's sister and her husband with my cousin Ari. And then standing in the center of the room talking to Rabbi Weiner was my dad. We met eyes. In a flash we were hugging, tight.

"You came!" I said.

"Of course I did." We pulled apart, and he was beaming ear to ear. He must've seen me glance around the room. "Don't worry," he said. "She's back in New York."

I smiled. "Great to see you, Dad."

"You, too, champ."

Everyone clapped, and just like that I was besieged by moist-lipped kisses and hearty handshakes. "Look how big you are!" they all said. "Quite a suit you've got!" they said. "What's with the shiner?" they asked, followed by "I bet the other kid looks even worse!" and then they laughed.

I heard a scream and turned to see my mom standing in the doorway, in complete shock and disbelief.

"Ruth!" everyone yelled, and her mother and father gave her a giant hug.

Pam was right behind, and through all the commotion I noticed her shoot my dad a quick wink. He winked back. That's when I realized that she had helped him set all this up. She'd broken my mom's no-family rule and hadn't told her.

Finally Patrice came in, followed by her dad, a tall, thin guy in a dark suit. As for Patrice, well, she was wearing a very pretty blue and white dress, and she had obviously spent a lot of time on her hair. She didn't look entirely comfortable, but she looked great. And I thought, Well, if my dad thinks that's my girlfriend, then he's gonna think I'm doing okay.

That was when the rabbi came over and put an arm around me. "Come on, Evan," he said, smiling. "It's time."

Mom and Pam had done their best to make the basement of the church look appropriate for a bar mitzvah. Four circular tables with chairs and place cards were set up in the audience. Hanging from the ceiling was a giant cutout of a Star of David. There was a makeshift bimah set up at one end of the room with four chairs and a rostrum with a microphone.

As Rabbi Weiner and I walked up, my dad went over to my mom and took her hand. She tried to resist, but everyone pushed her up to the stage with him. We must have looked awfully confused, me, Mom and Dad, sitting there in our chairs, pretending to be a family.

Or maybe not pretending.

Everyone quieted down and took their seats, and I finally had a chance to check out the rest of the decorations. There were flowers in the center of every table, and red tablecloths that matched the yarmulkes, and real china plates and silverware. I don't know where it came from or who paid for it, but it looked much better than I had ever imagined the church basement could look. On an easel in the corner was a blown-up picture of me as a baby, lying in a bathtub and laughing. And against the back wall was a table overflowing with food: deli trays, pickles, brisket, chopped liver, kasha. I looked at all that Jewish food and suddenly was struck with how much I had missed eating it.

Rabbi Weiner stood up, opened his siddur, and began chanting. He seemed more alive than I had ever seen him. Finally he was among his own people.

After a couple of prayers in Hebrew, he told everyone that they were all there to celebrate Evan David Goldman becoming a bar mitzvah, and he talked about how important it was that my family was there on this wonderful day. Up until today, he said, my parents had been responsible for me, and it had been up to them to make sure I followed Jewish laws and traditions. But now, today, I was a man, fully responsible for who I was and what I did.

"As you might have noticed from his right eye," the rabbi joked, "he's taking that responsibility very seriously."

Everyone laughed. Then the rabbi said it was time for me to read from the Torah. He pulled a large crate from underneath the rostrum, lifted a flap, and removed an object covered in blue velvet with Hebrew letters on it. Rabbi Weiner clumsily removed the velvet covering and lifted the scrolls up for everyone to see. My father and his sister's husband were called to hold the Torah and walk through the room, allowing everyone to touch it and say a prayer. Sitting at a table by themselves, Patrice and her dad weren't quite sure what to do when it was their turn. But then they both touched it, looked at each other, and shrugged.

When the Torah finally made its way back up to the bimah, my dad sat down next to my mom. It was a little bit awkward. I could see him looking at her, hoping for some sort of a connection. Finally she looked at him and smiled. Dad held her gaze for a split second before she looked away. It wasn't much, but since I knew how she felt, it was a pretty big gesture.

Then suddenly it was quiet, and I realized everyone was looking at me, including the rabbi. I got up and walked to the rostrum.

Looking out at the crowd, my eyes lingered on the ten empty spaces at Patrice and her Dad's table. And I never would have dreamed that I'd think this, but what went through my head at that moment was: I never needed those kids in the first place, and I'm glad they're not here.

I looked down at the Torah, assuming I'd see my portion there. But the Hebrew on the page of the Torah was written by hand and much more ornate. It looked entirely different from what I'd been working from. It didn't matter—I had memorized my part by now.

And so I sang:

כֹּה־אָמַ֞ר הָאֵ֣ל ׀ יְהֹוָ֗ה בּוֹרֵ֤א הַשָּׁמַ֙יִם֙ וְנ֣וֹטֵיהֶ֔ם
רֹקַ֤ע הָאָ֙רֶץ֙ וְצֶאֱצָאֶ֔יהָ נֹתֵ֤ן נְשָׁמָה֙ לָעָ֣ם עָלֶ֔יהָ
וְר֖וּחַ לַהֹלְכִ֥ים בָּֽהּ

When I had finished reading, I looked up at the rabbi, who smiled and nodded. And I looked at Patrice, who gave me a big thumbs-up. And I glanced at my mom and dad, both beaming and dabbing away tears.

Rabbi Weiner leaned into my ear and whispered, "Do you have the speech?"

I took a deep breath. My hands were shaking. The Hebrew was just memorization. But the speech had always been the hard part. And even though I had tried, I had never been able to get a good draft down on paper. Suddenly my heart was pounding hard.

"No," I said. "But I still have something to say."

He smiled, a big proud smile. "Then say it!"

With that, he went back to his chair.

There was my family, all gathered in this unlikely building in this unlikely town, and there was my one friend who had put up with me and stood by me, and there I was. I had survived the divorce and the move to Indiana. And in the process I had learned a whole lot about who I was. Maybe I could say something about that?

But just as I opened my mouth to begin, I heard a beeping sound. Then the basement door creaked and Archie's mother peeked in. Everyone turned to look. "I'm so sorry," she whispered, and she held the door open. There was a whirring noise and Archie came in, looking pale and sitting in a motorized wheelchair. He saw everyone staring at him, and I could tell he was mortified. Patrice immediately got up and moved a chair away from the table so Archie could sit there, and I realized that if I started talking, everyone would stop looking at him.

So I did.

This is what I said:

I'm supposed to talk about being a man today. The problem is that I don't feel much like a man. For the past two months, I haven't even felt like a person. I thought I knew what my life was, with my mom and my dad in our apartment in Manhattan and all my friends, and all that's changed now. Everything.

I guess I used to think that being a man meant that I would be old enough and smart enough to do anything. Like if I were really a man, I could just make everything go back to the way it was. If I were really a man, I wouldn't be in Appleton, Indiana. Or the star quarterback would be my best friend. And Mom would drive a BMW and live in a mansion. I'd be the Brain—the guy who knew everything, who everyone looked up to. If I were really a man, I wouldn't have to be different. I wouldn't even have to be Jewish. Anyway, that's what I used to think. That being a man means being able to make the bad things go away.

But if I can't make the bad things go away, what does that make me? In the last couple of months, I've realized that people are going to let each other down, people are going to lie, and people are going to get sick. And I can't stop any of that from happening.

It's weird. According to Jewish law, you hit thirteen and you're automatically supposed to be smart and responsible. You're supposed to

*know things. But I really don't have any
answers. Not good ones anyway.*

*But I'm here. I read the Hebrew. So I must
be a man now, right?*

*I didn't think you'd all be here today, but
now that you are, I'd like to ask you a favor
and I hope you'll say yes.*

*Walk behind me. Make it so that when I
don't know where to go, I can turn around
and you'll be there pointing the way. And if I
fall down, somebody just come pick me up,
and don't make me feel like I failed.*

*Because I pledge to you that I'm going to
try to be a man. I'm going to try as hard as I
can. But I'm going to need all the help I can
get. I think I can do it. But I can't do it alone.*

I looked out at my whole family, at my new friends,
at this whole cobbled-together version of my new and
old life. I heard my mother sniffle. Patrice and Archie
were both smiling at me. Rabbi Weiner put his arm
around my shoulders.

"Amen," he said, and everyone repeated it.
Amen.

THERE'S A lot of other stuff I could tell you—
about the Quails losing the championship after all;
about Kendra and Lucy getting in a fight when
Kendra got the lead in the musical and never talking
to each other again; about Angelina and my dad getting married.

I guess I could also tell you about how one night
over Thanksgiving break Patrice and I stayed up until
midnight playing Scrabble, and after she beat me for
the fifth time, I leaned over and kissed her—both lips.
And then I did it again.

But really, there's only one other story I want to
tell.

In the spring there was a talent show. And Kendra, of course, worked up a big dance number that everyone went nuts for. But then, right after her song, while she was still onstage, the band started playing a different tune, something slow and sort of mystical. And suddenly Archie wheeled himself out, carrying a microphone.

The audience went berserk, clapping and laughing. Then Archie turned to them and asked them to be quiet. Patrice was sitting a couple of rows ahead of me with her dad, and she turned and looked at me and I smiled.

Then Archie cleared his throat, and he sang the song I had heard on his computer six months before, the song that told Kendra that what he wanted more than anything else in the world was for her to notice him and know his name.

Blushing, Kendra stared out into the audience. We hadn't said a word to each other since Brett beat me up, but I wondered if she remembered what she had promised me.

When Archie was done singing the song, there was not a sound in the whole auditorium. Everyone was just staring at Kendra and Archie, lit by two spotlights alone on the stage.

Kendra got up and walked over to Archie's wheelchair. She smiled.

The crowd whooped and hollered. People started taking pictures with their cell phones.

Kendra kneeled down next to Archie and took his hand. He dropped the microphone and it landed with a thud. He was shaking.

Then Kendra took Archie's face in her hands, and turned it so he was directly looking at her. And there, in front of that whole room, the most popular and most beautiful girl in Appleton, Indiana, kissed Archie.

(But no matter what he tells you, there was no tongue.)

• • •

Listen to an exclusive mp3 of
Jason Robert Brown singing
"A Little More Homework to Do"
from the musical *13*. Just visit
www.harpercollinschildrens.com/13song
and enter this password
when prompted: INDIANA.

• • •